the
TRAPDOOR
mysteries

THE LOST TREASURE

THE TRAPDOOR MYSTERY SERIES

the TRAPDOOR mysteries

THE LOST TREASURE

ABIE LONGSTAFF

Illustrations by James Brown

Orion
Children's Books

ORION CHILDREN'S BOOKS

First published in Great Britain in 2019 by Hodder and Stoughton

3 5 7 9 10 8 6 4 2

A CIP catalogue record for this book
is available from the British Library.

ISBN 978-1-5101-042-66

Printed and bound in Great Britain
by Clays Ltd, Elcograf S.p.A.

The paper and board used in this book are
made from wood from responsible sources.

Orion Children's Books
An imprint of
Hachette Children's Group
Part of Hodder and Stoughton
Carmelite House
50 Victoria Embankment
London EC4Y 0DZ

An Hachette UK Company
www.hachette.co.uk
www.hachettechildrens.co.uk

To K & E

– A. L.

For Ivy xxx

– J. B.

The Secret Library's Rules:

There will be only one Secret Keeper
in each generation.

The Secret Keeper must be
under the age of thirteen.

The Keeper must guard the secret of
the library and the information within.

Talking is permitted.

CHAPTER ONE

Tally the servant girl was curled up in her bed in the scullery sink, her head right under the taps and her feet … wait. No. That's not right.

Tally sat up sharply. She wasn't in her sink bed anymore. She was in a luxury four poster bed, in the red bedroom of Mollett Manor. And she wasn't the servant girl any more. Now Tally was Lady Tallulah Mollett, daughter of Lord Mollett and niece to Lady Beatrice. It had only been three months since she'd told Lord Mollett that she was his daughter and, since then, everything had changed.

'Wuff!' Well, not everything. Widdles, Mollett Manor's mischievous puppy, still slept at her feet, and Squill, Tally's squirrel friend, still shared her pillow.

Squill yawned and climbed up Tally's nightdress on to her warm neck.

'Squill!' giggled Tally, 'You're tickling me!'

She swung her legs out of bed and on to the thick Persian rug. At the window she drew the curtains wide, letting the early-morning sun fill the room. From here she looked over the stables, past the apple orchard, beyond the stone circle, to the sea. The light sparkled and danced on the blue water.

Tally smiled. Life was almost perfect. *Almost.* There was just one thing – one person – missing. Ma.

Tally opened her wardrobe full of dresses. Beatrice Mollett had been so excited to find she had a niece.

'It's a girl!' she'd cried in joy. 'Oh, I can't wait to dress you up!'

She'd telephoned the dressmaker right away and, by the end of the first week of being a lady, Tally had more dresses and hats than she could possibly wear. Secretly, though, Tally still preferred her raggedy old dress and pinafore. The new dresses were beautiful, but they were not made for running or jumping or anything practical.

She fingered a bright yellow fabric. Lady Beatrice loved her in this dress. But it had no pockets! Where would Squill sit? *How do ladies carry anything useful on their person?* Tally wondered. She pulled the yellow dress down from the wardrobe, slipped it over her head and added a pinafore.

'It's a fair compromise, Squill,' she said, and the squirrel nodded in agreement. He scampered to a drawer and came back with a pair of stockings in his paw. Nowadays, Tally wore bloomers, and a petticoat and a garter belt under her dress. She'd never been so warm! She pinned the new silk stockings to the belt, which held them up.

'There!' she said, smoothing the dress down. 'Now let's look at our mural.'

As well as dresses, her aunt had insisted that Tally learn some more ladylike pursuits.

MRS PRIMM'S GUIDE TO BEING A LADY (Lady Beatrice's favourite book) was as helpful on the subject as ever.

Ladies may take up a range of gentle activities, it said.

Singing (but only quietly)
Sewing (but only neatly)
Dancing through flowers (but only slowly)
Painting (soft colours only)

Tally had chosen painting. The ancient monks of the manor had preserved their story in the tapestry hanging downstairs, and Tally had decided to paint her own journey – in the form of a mural on the corridor wall. She wanted to pay tribute to all the creatures who'd helped her. She'd stayed up late last night working on it.

'Come on, Squill. I want to see how the new

drawings look in the daylight.'

On the wall of the corridor was the start of an animal scene. Tally had used charcoal to mark out where the different creatures were to go. There on the top left were the spiders, who'd helped her learn the secret of spinning a web. Below them was a large bloodhound, his nose coming straight at the viewer. His ability to scent had inspired Tally to build a sniffing nose, which she still wore now and then for fun. Only last week, she and Squill had lain on their backs in the grass by the beehives, sniffing the warm, musky, waxy smell of new honey being made.

Tally ran her fingers over the outline of a gecko, a drawing of her friend who she'd saved from the Carriage of Curiosities.

'We haven't added enough detail here yet, Squill.'

He looked up from his spot on the floor, where he was painting a swipe of green on the mural with his fluffy tail.

'I really want all my animal friends in this painting but I can't get the gecko's toes right. And he keeps scurrying away every time I try to draw him ... I know!' She beamed. 'We'll go to the Secret Library! There's bound to be something about gecko toes there.'

'Wuff!' barked Widdles, wagging his tail excitedly.

Splodge!

Widdles knocked over the pot of green paint. It spread across the newspaper on the floor.

'Oops,' said Tally. She took a rag from her pocket and began to clean up.

'Morning!' Lord Mollett called. He rolled his eyes at the spilled paint and grinned at his daughter. Tally smiled back.

'Morning, Pa,' she answered. It had taken a while to work out what to call Lord Mollett. She couldn't call him 'My Lord' any more. 'Edward' felt strange, especially because Ma had called him 'Bear'. 'Daddy' felt odd too. Somehow, 'Pa' was the only one that was right.

'I'm going to go through the papers again,' he said. 'Come and find me in my study when you're ready. Hopefully I'll have some news for you.' Every day Lord Mollett looked through old newspapers from ten years ago, when Ma had fallen over the edge of a cliff. So far he hadn't found anything useful.

He crossed his fingers and held them up to show Tally. 'I know she's alive somewhere,' he said as he headed into his study. 'She has to be. And maybe I'll find her today.'

Click!

Lady Beatrice walked towards Tally, snapping a photograph. She lowered her camera and smiled at her niece. 'You look lovely,' she said.

'Thank you, Aunt Beatrice. I'm just going out for a walk.'

'Then will you paint a picture of Lord William on to the mural?' 'Lord William' was Widdles's real name: Lord William Horatio Mollett.

'Absolutely,' said Tally. 'Although he seems to be doing a good job on his own.' They looked at

Widdles, who was trying to get the green paint off his fur by pressing himself on the floor. There were now three green doggy-shaped prints on the white rug.

'Oh dear,' said Lady Beatrice. 'Mrs Sneed! Mrs Sneed!' She headed back down the corridor towards the servants' quarters to find the housekeeper.

'Quick,' Tally whispered to Squill. 'Let's go before Mrs Sneed comes. She's not going to be happy about all this mess.'

Tally dashed to the fireplace in her room. On the wall above it was a puzzle called a Magic Square. In every row, every column and every diagonal, the numbers had to add up to fifteen.

She pulled out the wooden blocks and moved them around until she had:

The door at the back of the fireplace clicked open and Tally and Squill slipped into a secret passage just as the housekeeper came along the corridor. Tally could hear her grumbling in her spiky voice.

'One, two, three prints. Why are there three doggy prints? We don't have three dogs. Are there more of you?'

'Ruff?' came Widdles's confused reply.

Tally felt her way along a dark passage inside the stone walls of Mollett Manor. The manor

was a magical place, full of secret passages
and hidden doors, and Tally had found all of
them! She'd solved the puzzle to open a hidden
cubbyhole in the ballroom, she'd cracked the
code to enter the lookout tower, and she knew
exactly how to get all the way around the manor
without seeing a single person.

In the darkness Tally stretched out her hands,
running her fingers over the stone wall till she
touched a lever. This opened the door at the end
of the passage. She stepped out into the fireplace

of the blue drawing room in the east wing.

From there it was easy. Down the stairs, into
the scullery and straight to another fireplace,
holding another puzzle. This one Tally could do
in her sleep. She'd used it so many times to sneak
to the Secret Library.

EXPERTS SNOOP was an anagram.
Rearranged, it spelled:
PRESS X TO OPEN.

On she went, through the tunnel under
the manor, and out into the fireplace in the
infirmary. From there, Tally simply opened the
door and she was in the grounds of the manor
house. She ran past the Malthouse, through the

apple orchard, all the way to the stone circle.

Here it was always quiet. Even the birds were hushed. This was a place of great magic and mystery. And, for Tally, it was a place of love. Ma had used this library too, until she was thirteen, and every time Tally set foot here, it was as if Ma was still with her.

'Oh Ma!' Tally breathed as she touched the velvety moss. She pictured Ma – Ma with her arms around her, Ma making up bedtime stories for her. Her favourites were the ones about a bear who escaped from the zoo. Ma used to draw him wearing different hats as he became a policeman or a schoolmaster. She'd even made Tally a little cloth teddy. But when Mrs Sneed had found Tally ten years ago, she had thrown the teddy over the cliff.

'I miss you, Ma!' Tally closed her eyes and wished for a moment on the stone monument; wished that her father would find something in the papers to help track down Ma; wished again for an answer to the questions which tormented her. Had Ma survived the fall from the cliffs? And if so, why hadn't she come back and found Tally? Tally pulled a scrap of lace from her pocket. This tiny piece of fabric came from the hem of Ma's skirt. It was all Tally had left of her mother. She swallowed hard and shook her head to chase the sadness away. She'd find out about the gecko and then go and see Lord Mollett.

The stone circle towered above her, five enormous rocks, weathered and ancient, cloaked in lichen and moss. Tally went to the central stone, the one with ten holes carved into the rock. This was the puzzle that opened the hidden trapdoor. Ten cubes had to be placed, each in exactly the right hole. There were millions of arrangements, called permutations,[1] but only one worked. Tally picked up the cubes. Each was carved with an image. There was:

[1] There are over three and a half million permutations. Tally has 10 choices of where to put the first cube, then 9 remaining choices for the second cube, 8 for the third and so on. If we multiply 10x9x8x7x6x5x4x3x2x1 we get 3,628,800 possible permutations.

A hand,

a stalk of grass,

a tree,

an hourglass,

a boat,

a sea,

a heart,

a bee,

a leaf,

and a gate.

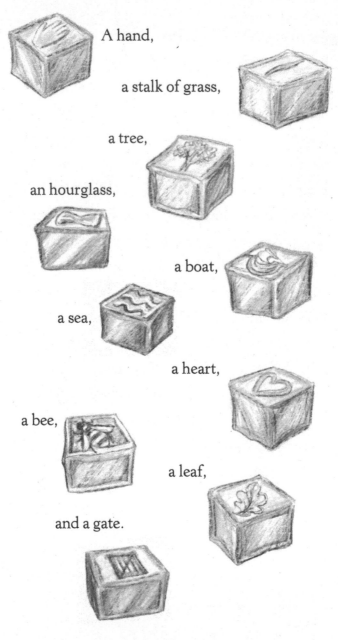

Years ago, Ma had taught Tally a song to remember the order of the cubes. By now, after three years of using the library, Tally knew where to put every cube. But she sang Ma's song anyway. It helped her feel closer to her mother.

Tally began to sing. As she sang, she put each cube in the right place.

Give me your hand and we'll run
Down past the grass, up through the trees
Give me your time and we'll sail
Down to the boat, up on the seas
Give me your heart and we'll fly
Up like a bee, down under leaves
This is the answer I know
This is the truth I will see
All the way down I will go
Down where the gate waits for me.

As she placed the last cube, there was a rumble in the earth at her feet. The ground shook and a piece of turf slid away to reveal a deep hole. Tally smiled. The entrance to the Secret Library was open!

CHAPTER TWO

Squill was always the fastest down the ladder to the bottom. He barely needed to use the rungs at all. He darted down the outside ropes, dancing his way to the ground.

'Light all the lamps,' Tally called into the hole. She turned and placed her feet on the first rung. She climbed down, down, down all the way to the last rung, then jumped off.

The library was bright and warm. She could see Squill at the back, lighting the final lamp. Tally looked up at the wonky shelves, twisting and turning up to the ceiling. Old ladders leaned against the wood, to help reach the uppermost books. Tally squinted to try to make out the ones

right at the top. She could see
the sparkle of gold lettering,
soft in the lamplight, but she
couldn't read any of the titles.

The books in the Secret Library
were ancient. They had been
here since the monks had made
this library back in the twelfth
century. A hundred years later,
in 1250, a wicked man had tried
to use the special knowledge
inside for evil. It was then that
the library entrance was sealed
to everyone except the Secret
Keeper. Nowadays, Tally was the
Secret Keeper. She had told no one about
the library, not even her father. It was her duty to
protect the secrets it contained.

Tally bit her lip as she walked past her beloved
books. She was twelve years old now. A Secret
Keeper had to be under thirteen years old.
That meant …

'Only a year left,' she said, sadly. It was going to be awful not having the magic of the library! How would she find out about how pond skaters glided on the water, or how bats used echolocation? There might be *ordinary* books on these things, in an *ordinary* library. But the Secret Library was *special*. It told Tally how to make all her inventions.

She stroked her finger over the dusty books. Their spines were cracked from use. Some were made of silk, some of leather. Some were tied with ribbon or twine. Others were bound with bluebell glue.

Tally walked

past the Bs

(BREAKFAST RECIPES by Hammond Deggs)

past the Cs

(CENTIPEDE LEGS by Adam Up

CHILDREN'S SONGS by Barbara Blacksheep)

and the Fs

(FLIPS AND CARTWHEELS by Jim Nastics)

all the way to the Gs.

There she found:

GECKOS AND LIZARDS by Sally Mander

The leather cover of the book was cracked and worn. It was dark red with silver decorations reinforcing the corners. It was held shut by two straps with gold buckles.

Tally sat down on a blanket, the book in her lap. Squill curled up beside her, playing with the yellow sash of her frock.

'Are you ready, Squill?' His body quivered with excitement, ripples running through his red fur.

Tally undid the buckles. They opened with a soft clink of metal.

There was a hush across the library. The lamps flickered.

'*A gecko is a kind of lizard,*' Tally read out loud.

Before her rose a hologram, a 3-D image. This was the magic of the library. Whenever Tally read out words from books, a moving image appeared before her. It even worked with Ma's diary! When Tally read Ma's words out loud, her image appeared, writing her diary at a desk in a room with yellow wallpaper.

Now, a small thin creature with a long tail rose up out of the book.
It scampered about on the shelves, darting up and down books, and in and out of shadows. The hologram was slightly transparent so, if she squinted, Tally could see through the gecko's body to  the library beyond. The hologram cast sunset across the floor, and the orange rays made the book titles glow golden.

Tally took out a notebook to scribble down facts for the mural.

'It says here that geckos normally live in warm places. That certainly explains why our one hangs out in the kitchen so much. I wonder how he got to England?' She turned a page.

'*Crested geckos come from New Caledonia,*[2]'

[2] New Caledonia was discovered in 1866.

she read. A globe of the earth appeared, showing the brown of the deserts, the green of the jungles and the white of the polar caps. The water shone and, when Tally peered closer, she could see the waves gently breaking on the shores. She reached out her finger to the water, but her hand slipped right through the hologram. The globe spun, moving past the deserts of the Middle East, over the Indian Ocean, past Australia to a group of islands.

'There's New Caledonia!' cried Tally.

'Zoologists sailed to the islands and brought back samples of animals and plants to Europe so they could study them.'

'Wow,' said Tally. 'Our crested gecko could have sailed all the way from New Caledonia on a ship. Imagine travelling that far! I'd love to go on a boat one day.' Tally grinned, her mind filling with images of all the places she could visit, all the things she could learn. The Secret Library was wonderful but Tally longed to see everything for *real*.

'Maybe one day, Squill.'

Tally turned the pages, making notes as she went.

'Ooh, Squill – geckos lick their eyeballs to keep them wet!'

The gecko crept out from the books and lazily flicked his tongue over his eye.

'Ew!' said Tally with a laugh. She skimmed the book to find the section on gecko feet.

'*The crested gecko has five toes,*' she told Squill, and the gecko held up a foot for Tally to see. On each toe there were little pads. Tally drew a little picture on her notebook to help her paint the gecko feet on the mural later.

'*Geckos can stick to any surface,*' Tally read out loud. The gecko ran up and down the library walls, over the shelves and even upside down! Then, just to show off a bit more, it hung from a book cover by a single toe.[3]

---

[3] Gecko feet can hold almost 400 times their body weight.

'Wow!' breathed Tally. Squill looked a bit jealous. Tally read on.

'For centuries people have marvelled at how the gecko can stick and unstick itself so easily. The stickiness of the gecko's feet could have many uses for human beings.'

'That's true,' said Tally. 'We could make a super sticky tape!'[4]

Just then there was the deep ring of a bell. It was the gate bell of Mollett Manor. The postman, thought Tally, cocking her head to the side, waiting to see if anyone would answer it. It rang again.

'Oh, I bet Mrs Sneed is still cleaning up after Widdles. And Mr Bood will be out in the new motorcar.'

Lord Mollett had ordered a brand-new engine for the family – their first motorcar! It had arrived only last week and Mr Bood had been given the task of learning to drive it.

---

[4] Tally is right – that could be useful. But even more useful would be sticking skin together after surgery or finding a way to make something sticky when it is under water or in outer space. Scientists are working hard on making an artificial gecko pad for precisely these uses.

'I'd better answer that bell myself, Squill,' said
Tally, closing the book with a sigh.

Tally carried a parcel from the postman up to
Lady Beatrice. On the way she stopped at the
tapestry hanging in the hallway. This was one
of her favourite things at Mollett Manor. It had
been woven hundreds of years ago and each
embroidered image was a clue to unlock the
trapdoor to the Secret Library. Every time she
passed it Tally was reminded of the ancient magic
of the manor house. She gave it a little stroke and
went on up the stairs towards the bedrooms.

As she approached the study, she heard Lord Mollett give a deep sigh. Tally gently pushed the door open.

'Are you all right, Pa?' she asked.

Lord Mollett had his head in his hands. He looked up at her voice.

'I can't find anything,' he said. 'Not anything in the whole of England.' He waved his arm over the piles of papers at his desk. 'How can there be no record of Martha at all? I've looked in every hospital record, every newspaper, every marriage register – nothing.'

Tears prickled at the back of Tally's eyes. She walked to the big leather armchair in the centre of the room and slumped down, with the parcel on her lap. Maybe Ma really was gone. Mrs Sneed had always said she'd died from the fall. Maybe she was right.

'Goodness.' Lady Beatrice breezed in. 'Everyone looks very miserable.' These days, she danced around the manor house in a state of extreme happiness. With her puppy and her photography, her time was filled with fun and jolliness. She picked up that day's newspaper.

'Gosh. I see why now,' she said, pointing to a headline. Tally read it over her shoulder.

BREAK-IN AT BRITISH MUSEUM

An Egyptian amulet was stolen last night.
Turn to p4 for the full story.

P10 BURGLAR FASHION OUTFIT INSPO	P12 CLEOPATRA – MY BATHING TIPS FOR BEAUTIFUL SKIN

'Artefacts are all the rage at the moment,' said Lady Beatrice. 'All the best country houses have them.' She sighed. 'I really wish Mollett Manor had some old pieces.' She looked at Tally. 'It's a shame there isn't anything ancient here,' she said sadly. Tally opened her mouth and then closed it again.

Lord Mollett closed the paper. 'They'll have trouble finding that amulet. By now it could be anywhere in the world. The thief will want to take it far away so he can sell it somewhere it isn't easily recognised – on a train or a boat or in a motorcar. Oh that reminds me. Mr Bood is supposed to take me on a practice drive.'

There was the crunch of gravel and Tally looked out the window. There below her was the brand-new motorcar. It was a Sunbeam car, very fancy and modern. Mr Bood was in the front, slowly steering it up the main drive, bumping up and down in the seat as he went. His chubby cheeks wobbled as the motorcar bounced and his hat nearly flew off his head in the wind.

Crunch! went the motorcar into the base of the fountain.

'Who put that fountain there?' came Mr Bood's cross voice through the open window.

'I'd better go and help him,' said Lord Mollett, grabbing his hat and driving gloves.

Lady Beatrice glanced at the parcel in Tally's arms. 'Are those my photographs?' She took the parcel eagerly. 'I've been waiting for these.' She sat on the study sofa and patted the cushion next to her for Tally to sit down.

'I went all around the village,' she told Tally, 'taking photographs of everyone. I'd never met the villagers before but they were quite lovely. Do you know, Tally,' she said, 'poor people are just like us, only with less money.'

Tally chewed the inside of her cheek to stop herself laughing.

Lady Beatrice tore open the parcel. 'Oh, wonderful!' she cried as she spread the photographs out on the low table. Her photography skills were improving by the day. Tally flicked through pictures of the local shops, the blacksmith's, the school house. Here was Adam in the blue house with his guinea pig, there was the postman and the doctor and—

'What a lovely photograph of Miss Carpenter,' cried Lady Beatrice, passing Tally another picture. Tally's heart jumped. It was a photograph of a lady standing in a cosy room. It wasn't anyone Tally knew. There was nothing special about the lady. It was the wallpaper behind her that caught Tally's eye.

Wallpaper with yellow birds on it.

Wallpaper she'd seen before.

Wallpaper just like Ma's.

CHAPTER THREE

There were butterflies flitting about in Tally's
tummy. Giant butterflies.

She tucked the photograph in her pinafore
pocket and closed the gate to Mollett Manor
behind her. Tally walked down the lane, along
the perimeter wall, past the church and school
and all the way to the park. Here stood a row of
three houses.

'Miss Carpenter lives at number three,' said
Tally, looking up at the doors. Squill nibbled her
ponytail and pretended he could read numbers.

There it was! The house had
a wooden door, with a brass
doorknocker shaped like a fox's head.

Tally took a breath and tried in vain to calm her butterflies. Not long ago, the Secret Library had shown her something amazing: a hologram of Ma! Ma was writing her diary in a room with yellow birds on the wallpaper. She might have been inside this very house! Tally bit her lip. She hadn't told Lord Mollett about her discovery, just in case she was wrong.

Lots of people have yellow wallpaper, she told herself, so as not to get her hopes up. But still her hand trembled as she lifted the fox head and rapped it on the door.

The door opened. It was the lady from Lady Beatrice's photograph.

'Yes?' she said.

'Miss Carpenter? I'm Tally, from Mollett Manor,' said Tally.

'Oh! Is it about my photograph?' said Miss Carpenter, fluffing her hair. 'Come in!'

Tally perched on the edge of the sofa, the photograph in her hand. Miss Carpenter was very excited.

'I've never had my likeness taken before!'
She flushed pink and her hands trembled as
she snatched the photo. 'Do I look like Auntie
Maud?' she asked, stroking the picture. 'Do I?'

'I'm not sure,' said Tally, who had never met
Auntie Maud. The question gave her a good
excuse to stare at Miss Carpenter, though. Tally
looked closely for any resemblance to Martha.
But Miss Carpenter was nothing like Ma. Ma
had curly hair, and a round, sunny face. Miss
Carpenter's hair was straight and thin and her
face was sharp and angular.

'Where was the photograph taken?' asked
Tally.

'Upstairs in the guest room,' Miss Carpenter
answered. 'Do you want to see? I've a painting of
Auntie Maud up there so we can compare.'

Tally followed Miss Carpenter up the stairs,
her heart was beating fast. Squill was excited
too. She could feel him wriggling in her pinafore
pocket. They turned left at the top of the stairs
and walked into a small bedroom …

'Oh!' Tally cried out. It was Ma's room! Just like she'd seen it in the hologram. She began to feel faint.

'Are you all right, dear?' Miss Carpenter said. 'You've gone quite pale. Here – sit down on the bed.'

'Thank you,' Tally replied. 'It is a lovely room,' she added, politely.

'I do like to keep it nice for guests.' Miss Carpenter looked at her intently. 'My dear, you remind me of someone, looking all pale and wan like that. She was a fainter, too. Right there on that bed. Now, don't fret – I'll pour you some water.'

Miss Carpenter chattered on as she rose to make good on her promise. 'It was about ten years or so ago. She was in a right state, she was. Yes, you do look a bit like her, with those curls and your green eyes ...'

Tally suddenly realised what Miss Carpenter was saying.

'A lady? Came here? Ten years ago?'

'Yes. She was soaking wet and all shivery. I can't remember her name now – Mary? Margaret?'

'Martha?'

'Yes, that's it!' Miss Carpenter clapped her hands.

For a moment Tally couldn't breathe. *Ma! She didn't die in the cliff fall!*

'Tell me more,' said Tally, urgently.

'Let's see ... it was late at night. I remember the doorknocker gave me a fright, banging and a-banging. There she was on the doorstep, wet and shaking. She was almost drunk with fever and cold, poor thing. "I came back," she said over and over. Then she said something about a baby and a cave – but there was no child with her.'

The sea cave! Tally had discovered it herself, quite by accident. It led from the bottom of the cliffs at Mollett Manor all the way under the village and through to the fields beyond.

'I helped her upstairs,' Miss Carpenter continued, 'and she fainted right there, right where you are sitting now.' Tally looked down where her fingers touched the bed.

'She had a fever for over four weeks. She hardly made sense the entire time. Talking about a bear, would you believe!' Miss Carpenter gave a little laugh. 'It was the typhoid, I think.'

'Typhoid! Did … did …' Tally could barely ask the question. 'Did she *die*?' Squill poked a little paw out of her pocket and stroked her wrist.

'Young lady! No guest has ever died under my roof,' Miss Carpenter retorted. 'I gave her chicken soup every day. My granny's chicken soup can cure anything. No, after four weeks she woke up. Turns out she was right. Not about the bear; about coming back. Her family used to live here. In this very house. They were Portuguese, I think. Something like that. Anyway – she said she'd grown up in this bedroom. In her fever, she'd come back to the only place she knew. Oh, my dear, you do remind me of her, did I tell you that?'

Tally put her hand to her chest. She stared at the window. This used to be Ma's room! She'd lived here as a little girl. Long ago, she'd written her diary looking out of that very window. From here she'd sneaked over to Mollett Manor to use the Secret Library and to see her friend, Edward Mollett – her 'Bear'. Then everything had changed. As soon as they found out she was pregnant, Martha's parents had moved away in a rush. Tally had found Ma's letter to Lord Mollett.

They are taking me away.
I have so much to tell you and so little time.

We are going to have a baby!
They want me to give it up, but I won't.
I'm going to keep it and one day, when I'm older, when they can't stop me, I am going to come back and find you.

That's why she'd brought Tally back to the manor ten years ago – to show her the stone circle. And to find Edward, Tally's father. Tally closed her eyes. She still remembered that day at the cliffs.

The wind was sharp, blowing Tally's curls around her face …

Ma smiling as she leaned over the edge to feel for her diary in the hole on the cliff face …

A stumble …

A scatter of pebbles …

Tally's tiny fingers reaching out to grasp her mother's skirt …

And Ma was gone …

All that was left was a scrap of lace in Tally's hand and a teddy on her lap.

No wonder Ma had come back to this house after her fall. It was the only place she knew well. But where was she now?

'When she was well again, what did she do?' Tally asked.

'When she was stronger, she insisted on going out – to your Mollett Manor, in fact. Then she came back all in a rush. I remember her looking terrible – worse than when she'd had the fever. 'The housekeeper hasn't seen her!' she said, though I could barely understand her over the sobbing and raving. In her arms she  had a little teddy – wet through and salty with seawater. "It was washed up in the sea cave," she told me. "She must have fallen after me." You see – she was quite mad.'

'Mad?'

'Oh yes, mad. But not dead,' Miss Carpenter repeated. 'Anyway, she left that very day.'

Tally's heart leapt. 'Where did she go?'

'Oh, I've no idea. The last thing she said was, "I can't bear to stay without her." I remember because she said it firmly and so clearly. That was the last I saw of her. Now, come and look at the painting of Auntie Maud. Then you can compare our likenesses.'

'It must have been Mrs Sneed who sent Ma away,' muttered Tally to Squill, as she walked back home. 'She's been the only housekeeper here for years. But why did she do it? Even Mrs Sneed isn't *that* mean.' Tally pushed the gate open and ran straight into the kitchen.

'Lady Twiddle!' said Mr Bood, who could never remember her name. He groaned and prised himself out of the armchair. 'I could drive you to the courtyard fountain and back in the new car, if you like.'

'Not now, thanks,' said Tally, robotically. She felt icy cold inside. 'Where's Mrs Sneed?'

Mr Bood nodded towards the scullery.

Mrs Sneed was stacking jars on shelves, shelves

over the very sink that used to be Tally's bed.
She'd slept there for nearly ten years, with only a
raggedy old blanket for warmth. For all that time
Mrs Sneed and Mr Bood had bossed her, making
her do chore after chore at the manor house.
Squill climbed on to her shoulder and stood there
with his arms crossed.

Tally swallowed hard. Now wasn't the time for
emotion. It was time for the truth. She spoke her
question to Mrs Sneed's back.

'Ten years ago, did a lady come to the manor
house asking about me?'

Mrs Sneed huffed and carried on stacking.
'There was some busybody who came. One of
those church ladies, I expect. She asked if we had
a child here at the manor house. I told her no,
of course.' Mrs Sneed wiped her hands on her
apron. 'It was none of her business.' She turned
to face Tally. 'She'd only have taken you away
to some workhouse. No,' she held up a hand to
Tally, 'you don't need to thank me. Although if
you wanted to, you could start by making four

batches of cherry biscuits.'

'She wasn't from the church,' said Tally, her voice trembling. 'That was Martha. She was my mother.' Tally fought to push her bitterness down. Fought not to scream at the unfairness of it all.

Mrs Sneed gasped. Her hands flew to her face. There was a very long silence. And then;

'Sorry about that,' Mrs Sneed muttered. 'I ... I was only trying to do what was best.'

She looked down and fiddled with a button on her blouse. When she spoke again, it was in a whisper. 'I didn't know she was your mum.' She quickly wiped her eye with the hem of her apron and coughed to clear her throat.

Tally watched the housekeeper. It was the first time Tally had ever seen her looking guilty, or ashamed. Mrs Sneed was struggling to put her crumpled face back to its spiky self.

Tally closed her eyes and gave a little sigh. *What's done is done*, she told herself. *The most important thing is to find Ma.* Squill chattered from her shoulder, as if he agreed. When Tally opened her eyes, Mrs Sneed's face was back to normal.

'So,' said the housekeeper, her voice louder now, 'in light of this, er … *misunderstanding* … maybe only make one batch of cherry biscuits, not four.'

'At least we know she survived her fall from the cliff,' said Tally to Lord Mollett. She was sitting on the sofa in his study, her heart pounding … *And at least I know she wanted me.* Tally didn't say this bit out loud – but it was going round and round in her head. Ma didn't run away. She didn't abandon Tally.

'But I've tried all the records. I can't find her,' said Lord Mollett.

Tally paced up and down the study, thinking. Squill frowned too, from his perch on the hat stand. He did a somersault round one of the hooks, in case that helped.

'Wuff!' said Widdles, encouragingly.

'"*I can't bear to stay,*"' said Tally. 'That's what she told Miss Carpenter. Ma wanted to leave. She wanted to go away.'

'Yes. I've looked at paperwork from all over the country.'

There was a moment's silence and then …

'What if she didn't stay in the country?' said Tally, slowly 'What if she really went away, far away?'

Lord Mollett stared at her. 'Southampton,' he said. He picked up the telephone all in a rush. 'Harbourmaster, please.' He fiddled with the base of the telephone as he waited. 'I need you to check the manifests of all outbound ships. I'm looking for a passenger, first name Martha. Would have been some time in the autumn of …'

'Grr-wuff!' Tally turned to see Widdles caught on the hat stand. He was balanced on top, having copied Squill. The whole stand was now wobbling back and forth with the weight of the little dog.

'Whoa!' Tally cried and rushed to rescue him.

'How did you even get up there?' she asked as she lifted him safely down. 'Ah!' Her keen eyes had spotted a clue: a pair of green pawprints on the sofa arm. 'You silly thing. Hat stands are designed for squirrels. Everyone knows that!'

Lord Mollett gave a cry. He slammed down the telephone. 'She went to America!' he said, his eyes shining. 'Martha went to America on the SS *New York*.' He stood up. 'She must have gone straight to the port and got on the first ship leaving the country. That's why I couldn't find her!'

'What do we do now?'

'We pack.'

'Pack?'

'Yes! I've booked us all on the SS *Voyager*.

It leaves tomorrow morning. It's the fastest way to get to America.' He picked Tally up in his arms. 'We're going to find her, Tally!' he cried. Tally's heart filled with joy as her father swung her round and round the room.

'Wuff!' said Widdles. He jumped up onto his hind legs to join in. 'Ru-uff!' he barked, tripping over his tail.

'Whoa!' cried Lord Mollett, as the puppy landed on his foot. He clutched Tally tightly as he stumbled towards the sofa.

Whump!

They landed in a heap on the old couch and Widdles leapt straight up on to Lord Mollett.

'Wuff!' he said proudly, from Lord Mollett's chest.

Tally burst out laughing. She hugged her knees tightly. She felt like happiness was exploding out of her. They were going to find Ma! From now on everything would be all right.

CHAPTER FOUR

Tally couldn't sleep. There was no point even trying.

A ship! Tomorrow she was going to Southampton in the motorcar then on to a real steamship, sailing all the way to America.

'Come on, Squill,' she said. 'Let's finish our mural. We still need to add Widdles and the gecko.'

Tally and Squill painted till the middle of the night. Tally carefully drew in the gecko's feet, using the notes she'd made in the Secret Library. Squill used white paint to help draw Widdles, brushing his tail over the dog's coat.

'That's great,' said Tally. 'I'll do his ears and eyes.'

Soon they were finished. Tally stood back to admire it.

'There,' she said. 'Now a bit of my story will always be here.'

She pulled the scrap of lace out of her pocket and rubbed it between her finger and thumb.

'I hope we find you,' she whispered to Ma.

There was a flicker from the hallway lamps, as if the ancient manor had heard.

The next morning, Mollett Manor was full of excitement.

In the courtyard, Lady Beatrice was trying to cram fourteen hats into her handbag.

Mr Bood was practising different faces in the hallway mirror, in case Lady Beatrice needed a photography subject. He was switching between 'angry', 'happy', 'sad' and 'shocked' so fast that he looked like he was about to be sick.

And Mrs Sneed was doing her duty by standing on the doorstep, eating all the remaining cherry biscuits.

Tally waited by the motorcar, her bag in hand. She had packed a few dresses, her lace from Ma's skirt and the special spider brooch Martha had made Lord Mollett many years ago. She turned in a circle, gazing at Mollett Manor. There was the fountain where she'd rescued Widdles from the water so many times; there were the beehives; and the roses. In the distance she could see the woods where she'd first met Squill. Nearly her whole life had been spent here. It was all she had known for the last ten years.

'Ready?' her father asked. He had a pile of newspapers under his arm and he was fiddling with them nervously.

'Are you?' Tally asked, and Lord Mollett fumbled, dropping the newspapers. Tally bent down to help pick them up. The headlines were still all about the museum break-in on Saturday night.

AMULET CLUE!

A sweet wrapper has been discovered at the scene of crime. "'Juicy Fruit" is an American chewing gum,' said PC Bobby.

'These sweets are not for sale in England.'
Police say they are now hunting for an American.

'The thief might not be an American,' said Tally, thinking it through. 'It could just be someone who has been to America. Or had a parcel from America.' But it looked like the police were keen on the American theme.

'We ask the country to be vigilant,' said PC Bobby. 'If you see someone waving the American flag or singing the US national anthem, contact us immediately.'
p7 – Our cut-out-and-keep guide to American sweets
p14 – Who wore it best: Mr Hershey or Mr Cadbury?

Lady Beatrice peered around to check there were no Stars and Stripes waving anywhere in the courtyard, then they all climbed into the Sunbeam.

Tally sat in the back with Mrs Sneed and Lady Beatrice.

'I hope I've packed enough hats, Tally,' said Lady Beatrice. 'MRS PRIMM'S GUIDE TO BEING A LADY says you need one for every occasion.' Mr Bood handed Widdles to her and the little dog walked around her lap, putting muddy pawprints on her dress.

Squill was sulking inside Tally's new cloth bag. Lady Beatrice had been very clear: Tally was not allowed to wear a pinafore in public.

'What would people think?'

So she'd given her niece an embroidered drawstring bag to carry on her person.

It felt surprisingly heavy.

'I think you've been eating too many cherry biscuits,' Tally whispered to the squirrel.

Vrrrrmvrrrrrmvrrrrm! The engine rumbled like a tiger. The motorcar jerked forward, swung wildly to avoid the fountain, and headed down the main drive, with only two accidental stops and one last-minute swerve out of the way of a pothole.

'You're really getting the hang of it, Mr Bood!' said Lord Mollett in admiration.

As they swept through the gates of Mollett

Manor, Tally looked back. The house gleamed in the sunlight, looking elegant and stately. Nothing could be seen of the magic within: the coded fireplaces, the hidden tunnels and the Secret Library.

'See you soon,' Tally whispered, as they turned on to the open road.

Tally gripped the base of her seat with both hands as they bounced, bumped and swung their way into Southampton. Tally had never been to such a big city. In her village, theirs was the only motorcar. But here Tally saw *twelve* of them!

Lady Beatrice had her camera round her neck and was taking photographs of everything in sight.

'Please sit down, Aunt Beatrice,' pleaded Tally,

as she stood up yet again to photograph a
horse.

'Watch out!' cried Lord Mollett, and everyone
was crushed to the left as Mr Bood turned
abruptly, just in time to avoid a tram.

'Oh my days!' cried Mrs Sneed. 'Tally, make us
all a cup of tea!'

'I can't right now,' said Tally, holding on for
dear life as Mr Bood steered suddenly to the
right ...

'Lamppost!' warned Lord Mollett.

... and to the left.

By some miracle, they reached the dock in one
piece, with only two lost hats and one missing
bow tie.

The pier was crowded with people.

'Surely they won't all fit on our ship,' said
Tally.

'Some of them are here to wave loved ones off;
some are just here to see the ship,' Lord Mollett
explained.

'Aunt Beatrice! Careful!' cried Tally as Lady

Beatrice leaned far out of the car to photograph a small child waving a handkerchief.

Mr Bood steered into the crowd, honking his horn. Before him, people scattered out of the way of the large Sunbeam. They turned right onto the dock, and there it was! The S.S. *Voyager*.

Tally gasped – it was enormous! The dark grey hull towered over them and Tally had to tilt her head all the way back to get a proper look.

'Ow!' Mrs Sneed tilted her head back down and cracked her neck.

Creeaaack craaaack.

Mr Bood climbed out and began to lift down the luggage.

'Twooly – take all these bags!' he cried, before remembering that she wasn't a servant any more. 'I mean ... Lady Twooly ... Twilly ... Tworly ...'

Click! Click! Snap! went Lady Beatrice's camera.

'My goodness,' came a voice, 'is that the new Goerz?' A man gazed at Lady Beatrice's camera. He was dressed in simple style – just a shirt, waistcoat and trousers, rather than the fancy suit and hat Lord Mollett was sporting. He was clearly not a first-class passenger.

Lady Beatrice hesitated, then replied nervously. 'Why, yes,' she said.

'How do you find the shutter speed?' he asked. 'What about the focus? Oh, forgive me. I'm Charles Jones. I have so many questions about your camera.'

Lady Beatrice turned pink, happy to be asked about her craft.

Tally left her in conversation and went to help Lord Mollett with the tickets.

'That's three in first class and two in second,' said the steward. His name badge read 'Allsop'. His eyes flicked over the luggage. 'I'll help with those,' he said, reaching for the handbags and purses. He held out his hand for Tally's cloth bag.

'This stays with me,' she said firmly.

Allsop narrowed his eyes for a moment, then replied, 'Very well, my lady.'

Tally felt a burst of excitement as she stepped up on to the gangplank. Her first trip abroad!

'Wuff!' Widdles came running towards her. He was headed straight for the narrow gangplank. He was going to make it ... He *was* ...

He *was*...

He wasn't.

Splash!

'My puppy!' cried Lady Beatrice, as Widdles struggled in the sea.

Charles leapt off the pier and dived straight in the water.

'Ohhh!' a lady screamed, and the crowd rushed to look over the edge. Lady Beatrice rubbed her hands together anxiously. Moments later Charles popped his head out of the water, holding Widdles in one arm.

With his other arm, he swung himself back on to the dock using the gangplank ropes.

The crowd cheered. Widdles jumped down to run to his mistress, falling over his ears on the way.

'Ah, whoops. I think I've ruined my new shoes,' said Charles. He laughed and pulled them off.

Lady Beatrice put her hand on her heart and stared up at Charles. 'Thank you,' she said. Tally watched the two grown-ups gazing into each other's eyes.

Charles gave a little bow. 'At your service,' he said, gravely, and, dripping wet, he walked on to the gangplank.

Lady Beatrice blushed and gave a little cough.

'Goodness,' she said. And again: 'Goodness.'

Her eyes followed Charles all the way, as he disappeared into the ship.

CHAPTER FIVE

Tally followed Allsop down the corridor,
holding Widdles by the lead. The steward was
whistling a catchy tune as he walked, his arms
full of handbags and purses. He was dressed
immaculately in his bright white uniform, not
a hair out of place. Tally looked down. Even his
shoes were super shiny. One of them still had the
shop tag on it.

'This here is the grand staircase,' said Allsop.
'To your left is the barbershop, to your right the
gymnasium. Straight ahead are the dining rooms.
Your cabins are on B deck, the first-class section.
I will be your steward. I look after cabins B50 to
B60.'

Tally stepped on to deep, soft carpet. The
walls were made of shiny wood and there were
beautiful vases filled with flowers. Down the
corridor they went, all the way to the end.

Allsop handed Tally the key to cabin B58.
'You are here, my lady, with your family in the
cabins either side.' Tally clutched her cloth bag
under her arm, and there was a little squeak from
somewhere in the fabric.

'Thank you,' she said quickly. She opened the
door and shut it behind her.

Her cabin was enormous. The walls were
panelled in white wood, with decorative golden
designs on every archway. On her bed was a
silk counterpane (which Widdles was already
rolling on) and, best of all, she had her own little
balcony! She ran to it and threw open the heavy
curtains. The sea was far below her. She leaned
over, looking down to the water, then back to her
cabin.

It was such luxury, she could hardly believe
it. All the way from her sink bed to here, on the
grandest ship in the world.

'I really *am* a lady now!' she said with a smile as she did a wobbly little pirouette. There was a chatter of agreement and she turned to see Squill jumping from the side table to the armchair.

'Ruff!' echoed Widdles.

Squeak! came a voice from the cloth bag. Out popped a little pink rat's nose.

'Brie?' said Tally. 'What are you doing here?' The rat was swiftly followed by the gecko, who made his way to a patch of sunlight straight away. 'No wonder my bag was so heavy!' Tally laughed. 'It looks like everyone has come for the ride.' She filled a little saucer with water for the gecko and gave Brie a cup of her own.

'I'll bring you food whenever I can,' she told them. 'There's bound to be something wonderful to eat on this ship.'

She threw herself backwards on to her

silk sheets and swished her arms up and down the smooth fabric. Widdles barked and thumped his tail on her pillow.

'Ugh, Widdles! You're still wet from the sea.'

Tally pulled a brush from her bag. 'Keep still,' she said, as she ran the brush over the dog's knotty fur. How did he manage to get so tangled? She'd brushed him so much, the dog brush was full of fur that had begun to split into clouds of thin, dusty hair. Tally pulled the fur out of the brush and threw it in the bin.

'There. That's better.' Widdles jumped off the bed and lapped up the gecko's water.

Squill tutted at him. He leapt from the armchair to join Tally on the bed.

'Just think, Squill. All this glamour and adventure AND we're on our way to find Ma!'

Tally stroked his back, bumping her fingers along his spine. 'Do you think she'll recognise me?' she asked him. 'Do you think she'll know who I am?' Her voice grew smaller. 'Do you think she'll still want me?' Squill shot upright in outrage. He chattered loudly as if to say, *Don't be ridiculous.*

'But she might have married someone. She might have a new family now. Other children.'

Squill patted her wrist. But it didn't help.

'Come on, Squill,' said Tally. 'We can't sit here feeling sorry for ourselves. Let's go and explore.'

They spent the rest of the afternoon exploring the ship. It was huge. There was room for over a thousand people and the corridors turned this way and that, holding hundreds and hundreds of cabins.

'I hope we find our way back to cabin B58,' said Tally. Squill poked his head out of her bag to help memorise the way.

There was a shudder from the engines.

'We're leaving England!' Tally ran out on to the deck and leaned over the white railings.

The pier
was far below
her, packed with people
waving handkerchiefs.

'Goodbye!' Tally shouted down, and
the people waved and cheered.

'How terribly vulgar,' said a sharp voice.

A woman stood near the door to first class. She
wore a brown fur stole around her neck, so that
the head of a mink[5] sat on one of her shoulders
and its hind legs on the other. Tally shuddered.

'Don't you ever shout to the commoners like
that, Viola,' the woman said to a girl by her side.

'Of course not, Mother,' said Viola. Viola was
wearing a white lace dress. She had a bonnet tied
under her chin and shiny white shoes with blue
ribbons.

[5] A mink is a mammal. It is semi-aquatic, which means it
spends some of its time in the water.

Embarrassed, Tally smoothed down her dress where Widdles had dropped hair on it and began inching away from the pair, tucking one muddy boot behind the other until she had disappeared round the corner.

She headed across the deck, dodging a small boy with a hoop and stick. At the end of the deck was a flight of stairs. From up here Tally  could see Charles, the man who had rescued Widdles. He had set up a tripod with a large box camera balanced on top. He was taking a picture of people playing quoits. He angled the box into place to catch an image of one of the hoops flying through the air.

Tally climbed down the stairs and found Mrs Sneed, sitting in an armchair.

'Oh there you are!' she said as if she'd been off searching for Tally all afternoon. 'Are there any biscuits?'

Tally approached a nearby steward and came back to report. 'He's gone to get some.'

'Huh,' sniffed Mrs Sneed as if that really wasn't good enough. 'In the manor house I used to ask for biscuits and they'd arrive a second later.'

'That's because I always got up at dawn to make them,' Tally reminded her.

'Well, you were such a little thing. You didn't need much sleep anyway.' Mrs Sneed waved her hand, brushing away years of neglect and bossiness.

The steward arrived with a plate for Mrs Sneed. She took a bite.

'Oh no, no, no,' said Mrs Sneed. 'These are no good at all. My Tally makes far better biscuits.' Her voice was full of pride. Tally glanced at her in surprise. *My Tally?*

'She's the best little worker in the world,'

Mrs Sneed added, pushing herself up from the deckchair. 'Now you take me to the chef right away. I need to have a word. And a cup of tea. And on second thoughts, I'll just eat a few more biscuits to check they are as bad as I first thought.'

Tally left her heading towards the kitchen. *That poor chef.* She shook her head.

Squill climbed out of the bag on her lap and swung himself round and round the bars of the deckchair.

'Oh, you little cutie,' said a lady. 'What an unusual cat.'

'He's a squirrel,' explained Tally.

'Come here, little kitten,' said the lady. She held out a biscuit to Squill and he ran to take a nibble. 'There you go, puss.' She held up her knitting. 'I'm going to make your kitty cat a little hat.

It'll be cold when we get to Iceberg Alley.'

'Iceberg Alley? What's that?' asked Tally.

'It's by Newfoundland,' the lady explained. 'I take this voyage every year to see my grandchildren and every year we see enormous icebergs floating by.'

'Really?' Tally shivered. For a moment she had visions of hitting an iceberg, the ship sinking, her own body falling into the deep, deep, icy cold.

'Did you know that only the tip of the iceberg is above the surface?' said the lady, not helping Tally's momentary panic. Tally shook her head.

'They're very deceptive. Most of the ice is underwater, where we can't see it. My granddaughter told me that,' said the lady. 'She's studying to be a marine biologist.'

A marine biologist! Tally's eyes widened. 'Imagine working with creatures under the sea,' she said in amazement.

'Would you like to work with animals?' asked the lady.

'No,' said Tally. 'I'm going to be an inventor.' It was the first time she'd said it out loud. She pressed her fingers to her mouth, as if she'd said something very silly. But the lady smiled.

'Good for you,' she said. 'I'd have loved to have had a job. But it wasn't done in my day. You go ahead and invent things. I'll make your little kitten a hat.'

'The trouble is, Squill,' said Tally as she walked along the promenade, 'if I don't have the Secret Library, how can I invent things? It was the library that told me what to do.' She stroked the red bushy tail curled around her finger. 'Without it, I'm lost.'

Tally fiddled with the tablecloth. She was sitting in the first-class dining room and it was all very grand. At home the Molletts ate simply, just the three of them (well, four if you counted Widdles. And Squill … all right five of them.) Now the table was filled with smartly dressed diners: lords and ladies, barons and baronesses, dukes

and duchesses. *I'm a lady too*, Tally reminded
herself. *I have as much right to be here as they do.*
But inside she didn't believe it.

There were three knives at
her place, and three forks.
She flicked a glance at Lady
Beatrice and saw her pick
up the broad knife for her
salmon. Tally did the same.

'Wow,' she said. 'What a lot of
silverware to have to polish.'

There was a silence at the table. Viola and
her mother, Mrs Montgomery, stared at Tally
in horror. But Lord Mollett laughed. 'You are
absolutely right, Tally,' he said. 'We really don't
need all these knives and forks. One set will do.'
He leaned over and placed his extra cutlery on
the waiter's tray.

'I think it's good to keep servants busy,' said
Mrs Montgomery. 'It stops them getting up to
mischief. Just think of all the naughty things
they would do otherwise. I mean, did you see the

newspaper this morning? The police still haven't caught that museum burglar.'

'The amulet was only taken on Saturday night,' said Lord Mollett reasonably.

'It's Monday!' Mrs Montgomery said in outrage. She jabbed her finger on the tablecloth. 'How many Americans can there be?' *Jab. Jab.* 'All the police have to do is round up all the lower-class ones.'

Lady Beatrice lifted her camera and snapped a picture of Mrs Montgomery mid-rant.

'Oh!' cried Mrs Montgomery in surprise, her mouth a perfect circle. *Click!* went Lady Beatrice's camera.

After dinner Lord Mollett and Lady Beatrice went to the first-class lounge to play cards. Tally strolled on deck, breathing in the fresh night air. She leant over the railing and watched the moonlight playing on the very tips of the waves as the ship powered through the water. Squill yawned on her shoulder.

'I'm sleepy too,' said Tally. 'Let's go back to our cabin.'

It took Tally ages to find cabin B58 again. She went down corridor after corridor on B deck, looking at door after door.

'We're not in the right section at all, Squill,' she sighed as they passed Suite B72. They turned another corner. Walking ahead of them was Allsop. Something in his manner wasn't right. He was looking furtively from side to side. He seemed *sneaky*. Tally hung back. At the end of the corridor he looked left and right. Tally popped back behind the corner. When she dared look, she caught a last glimpse of Allsop slipping into one of the cabins.

'What is he doing here so late at night?' she asked Squill. 'He's not the steward for this section. He said he's supposed to be in our section – cabins B50 to B60.' Seconds later, the door opened again. Tally peeked out to see Allsop closing the door behind him. The steward stopped for a second and …

Atchoo!

He sneezed and pulled a handkerchief out of his pocket to blow his nose. He looked from side to side quickly, his face panicked.

Tally ducked back. When she looked next, he was gone. She heard him whistling his tune once more, after he'd safely rounded the corner, getting quieter and quieter as he walked away.

'Something did not look right about that,' she mused. She walked up to check the cabin number: B90. She looked down. There on the floor was a bit of paper.

'This must have fallen from his pocket when he got out his handkerchief,' she said.

It was a shop receipt for a pair of shoes bought today in Southampton.

'Well, that's not particularly strange,' said Tally, a little disappointed. 'He bought new shoes today. So what? Charles had brand-new shoes too. He said so.' She kept the receipt anyway, just in case.

Ahead was a set of stairs that brought her up

and round to the grand staircase.

'Oh yes,' she said. 'I know my way from here. My corridor is just to the left.'

But tucked up safely in bed, Tally still couldn't get to sleep. It was partly excitement, partly worry. The engines hummed, the ship creaked, Widdles snored (although that wasn't new). Thoughts kept buzzing around her head. She turned over in bed. She hadn't closed her curtains and the stars were winking through the porthole. *Was Ma looking at them too? Where was she? The plan had seemed so clear – go to America, find Ma. But America was a big place! Ma could be anywhere.* Now, looking up at the night sky, Tally felt tiny and powerless; a little drop in a huge ocean.

Fnufffle.

Widdles snorted and put his head on her feet. Squill nestled closer into the back of her neck. Slowly Tally calmed, and drifted off to sleep.

CHAPTER SIX

The next morning, Tally and Lady Beatrice went
for a stroll on the ship's deck. Mr Bood waddled
behind them. He was having a little trouble
finding his sea legs. His enormous tummy made
it tricky for him to balance, and he wobbled this
way and that as he walked, tripping over Widdles.

'Sorry!' he said, as he nearly fell into the lap of a
lady reading.

'Mr Bood, try to keep up,' said Lady Beatrice,
leading the way down a set of steps. 'What do
you think, Tally? Shall we take the view from the
second-class deck? Hmm?'

'Second class, my lady? Why's that?' Mr Bood
enquired.

'Oh, no particular reason. No person … I mean, reason, at all.' Her eyes scanned the deck, until… 'Why, look, Tallulah! There's that man who rescued Widdles. Oh, I can barely remember Charles's name. I mean, his name. I can barely remember his name. What is his name, Tally?'

'It's Charles,' Tally replied with a smile. 'Charles's name is Charles.'

Charles was balancing his box camera on top of a tripod, looking out towards the sea.

'Good morning,' said Lady Beatrice, primly.

His face lit up. 'Pleased to see you again. Come and see my new camera,' he said. 'My friend

Kaz[6] made it. He thinks it will be the future of filming.'

'Are you taking a photograph of the sea?' Tally asked.

'In a way,' he said, 'but

[6] Kazimierz Prószyński was one of the pioneers of movie making. He invented a number of film cameras, including the Aeroscope. Many years later, Kazimierz died in a concentration camp in Germany.

this is a moving photograph. One day, when I've saved up enough money, I'm going to open my own moving pictures company,' he added dreamily.

Mr Bood's eyes lit up. 'You could film me moving right now!' He leaned against the railings to get in shot. Then he put one foot on the bottom rung and the other one higher. He coughed and put on a deep booming voice as he quoted, 'To be or not to ... er, something or other.'

'Be?' suggested Tally, helpfully.

'Bee? Arghhh! Where?' Mr Bood looked around wildly.

'Careful, Mr Bood, you'll fall off!' warned Tally, grabbing his arm as he leaned further and further over the railing to get away from the non-existent bee.

'Stop it, Twilly. I want to make my speech,' said Mr Bood.

'Not much point,' answered Charles, cheerfully. 'My camera can't record sound. Just images.'

Charles showed Tally how the device worked and soon Lady Beatrice took over, moving the camera herself, focusing in on the moving waves.

'You're a natural,' Charles smiled warmly at her. Lady Beatrice beamed.

'Wuff!' Widdles jumped up to make sure he was getting enough attention. Charles bent down and patted his ears. Widdles rolled on his back for a tummy tickle.

'He'll keep you here all day, doing that,' Tally warned him.

'I don't mind,' he laughed. 'As long as I have company.' He looked right at Lady Beatrice. Tally smothered a giggle.

Widdles woofed in joy. His eyes were closed and the sunshine picked up the sparkles in his diamond collar, sending teeny rays of light across the deck.

The back of Tally's neck prickled and she turned to see Allsop. He was standing holding a tray of drinks, but his eyes were fixed on Widdles, staring straight at the collar.

'Hi there!' a passenger hailed the steward. 'Are those our drinks, Allsop?'

Allsop gave a little jerk. The tray wobbled as he turned to serve his customers.

Tally frowned. She wandered to a nearby deckchair and lifted a paper from its seat. It was the ship's own little newspaper.

ATLANTIC BULLETIN
from the Marconi room[7]
Police discover new clue in amulet case!
Ticket stub found at British Museum

Police say the thief must have used the second part of the
ticket to travel to Southampton after the crime.
They are now searching every house in that city
for an American.
p6—Could you be the burglar? Take our in-depth quiz
to find out
p8 —Southampton to London: make our knitted map
(free pattern inside)

---

[7] In 1901 Guglielmo Marconi sent the first transatlantic
signal from Cornwall to Newfoundland, allowing messages to
be sent and received. By 1907, a regular transatlantic radio-
telegraph service had begun.

'Southampton?' said Tally, as she sat down. 'That's where we got on this ship.' She thought back to Lord Mollett's words … *The thief will want to take the amulet far away so he can sell it somewhere it isn't easily recognised.*

A chill ran down her spine.

'Squill, this ship is the fastest way to get to America. What if the thief is on board, taking the Egyptian amulet to America to sell it?'

Squill chattered in outrage.

Tally scanned the deck. Everything seemed normal. Children were playing, people were dozing on deckchairs.

Tally watched her aunt talking to Charles. Lady Beatrice was talking so fast, her hands waving as she described her love of photography. Charles was leaning in, keen to hear more. Widdles was in his arms and Charles was playing with the puppy's diamond collar. Lady Beatrice seemed so happy talking to him! Tally smiled. Lady Beatrice had been unhappy for so long, ever since the Duke of Swantingdon broke off

their engagement twelve years ago. Lady Beatrice
had been humiliated, and had hidden away in
the manor, afraid to host parties or to see anyone.
Maybe there was a chance she could finally put
the past behind her?

'Let's leave Aunt Beatrice and Charles to get to
know each other, Squill,' she said. 'What say you
and I go and do a little snooping? We could see
if anyone looks suspicious. Maybe we'll find the
museum thief!' She was just about to get up when
she heard a voice.

'There's something not proper about that
Mollett family.' Mrs Montgomery spoke sharply
from the first-class deck above. Tally froze. Did
she know Tally could hear her from down here?
Evidently not, because Mrs Montgomery carried
on talking.

'The sister is talking to the riffraff, the brother
is clearly mad ... and that girl! Did you see her last
night, Viola? Her hair is a mess. And she really
should be wearing a corset. She's a disgrace.' Her
voice faded as the pair walked away.

Tally felt hot with shame.

'I've no idea how to behave at all,' she told Squill as her eyes filled with tears. 'No idea how to be a lady, how to act or how to dress.' Squill climbed on to her shoulder and patted her head as she sobbed. She felt all alone out here at sea. Pa was busy sending marconigrams from the ship to all over America, in hopes of finding Ma; Tally had no Secret Library to go to; no Mollett Manor to explore. Everything that moored her in place, all the world she had ever known, was far away.

Just then Mrs Sneed walked by. 'What's going on here?' she said. 'No point in snivelling when there's work to do. That kitchen could use a decent cook if you ask me. I've a good mind to send you over there to help.'

Tally lifted her head. 'It's that Mrs Montgomery. She thinks I'm not good enough to be a lady.'

'Humph,' said Mrs Sneed. She sat down in a deckchair next to Tally. There was a long silence then the housekeeper spoke again.

'I've met a lot of ladies, and you are an unusual one, it's true. You're not exactly graceful and neat, are you?' She gave Tally a stern look. 'But there's nothing to say you can't be your own special kind of lady. A clever one. You've solved every problem at the manor house. And on your own too. All that is much more useful than grace.' She crossed her legs. 'I never went to school myself. My brothers did but I started working at the manor house when I was just a girl. I often wonder what it would have been like to have had choices; if I could have shaped my life my own way.' She patted Tally's knee lightly. 'Now, I'm off to give that chef a piece of my mind. Again. And I won't let him sweet-talk me this time.' She pushed herself out of the deckchair and walked away towards the kitchens.

Tally stared after her in shock. This was probably the most kindness Mrs Sneed had ever shown her.

'Yoohoo!" came a cry, as the knitting lady plomped herself down in the deckchair next to

Tally. 'Where's that kitty cat of yours? I've made him a lovely hat.'

Tally could feel Squill burrowing deeper into the cloth bag on her arm as the lady held out a purple and green stripy hat. It had a bobble on top and a pretty lace brim. Squill was going to hate it.

'Guess what I found for him too,' the lady went on. 'Blackberries! Chef gave me—'

Squill didn't even wait for her to finish her sentence. At the scent of blackberries, he shot out of Tally's bag.

'There you are!' said the lady. Squill jumped on to her wrist and was so happy eating that he didn't even notice her slip the bobble hat on to his head. 'You look so sweet, puss.' She picked up her wool. 'I'll make him booties next,' she told Tally. 'Here,' the lady added. 'Have a sweet. I love these American candies. I get a big bagload every time I go to New York.' She laughed and gave Tally a little chocolate wrapped in silver foil, before wandering off again.

Tally unwrapped it and popped it into her mouth, but she was frowning as she watched the woman walk away. *American sweets. That's what the police found at the museum crime scene. Surely she couldn't be the burglar?* Her mind worked hard to picture the old lady, waiting outside the museum in the middle of the night, eating American sweets.

'She could have asked someone else to steal the amulet, Squill. We can't discount her just because we like her. Remember what she said about icebergs, Squill. "*They're very deceptive. Most of the ice is underwater, where we can't see it.*" Maybe she is a bit like an iceberg herself?'

Squill nodded so firmly that the bobble hat slipped over his eyes. He pushed it up with his paw, then huffed crossly when it fell down again. Tally laughed.

'It's your own fault,' Tally said to Squill. 'You're the one who came out of the bag for a blackberry. Now you're going to have to wear that hat every time you see her. It's no use sulking. You know you have t—'

But before Tally could finish her sentence, a siren split the air. It was loud and sharp in the peace of the day.

Wooo-ooo-wooo-ooo!

'Quick, Squill, we'd better go and find the others.'

Spotting them in the distance, Tally rushed

over to Lady Beatrice and Mr Bood. 'We need to go to the muster point,' she said urgently.

'What's that, Lady Twoodle?' asked Mr Bood.

'Do you remember I told you about muster points?'

'Like it was yesterday.'

'It was this morning,' said Tally. 'Just as we walked across the promenade.'

'Oh. Then no.'

'We need to go back to our deck to gather together,' she explained, waving him on. He wobbled off.

Tally took her aunt's arm.

'What's happening, Tally? Is there something wrong?' Lady Beatrice asked.

'I don't know,' Tally answered honestly. 'But it doesn't sound good.'

They joined the other passengers on the first-class deck. People were muttering and complaining.

'The sea is perfectly calm,' said a man. 'I don't know why they called us up here.'

'I was in the middle of a bridge game,' a lady grumbled.

'I hope there's not an iceberg ahead,' said another lady.

Captain Roberts strode on to the deck and stood in his white uniform and hat to address the passengers.

'Ladies and gentlemen,' he said in a loud voice. 'I'm afraid I have very grave news.' He took a deep breath. 'There is a THIEF on board!'

There were gasps from the crowd.

A thief! Tally looked at Squill in excitement. Was the captain talking about the Egyptian amulet? Had he already found the museum burglar?

'Miss Davenport's rubies have been stolen from her cabin!' said the captain. Every first-class passenger lifted a hand to their necklace or watch to check it was still there.

'A second thief on the ship?' Tally whispered to Squill. 'That would be a big coincidence. I wonder … maybe the same person took the amulet AND the rubies?'

Squill frowned thoughtfully.

'Do not be alarmed,' said the captain. 'We are taking this very seriously. We won't stop until we have returned the jewels to cabin B90.'

Tally put her hand to her mouth – B90! But that was where she had seen Allsop last night!

The captain carried on. 'We ask that everyone

remain here while the ship is searched. It may take some time so luncheon will be served out here for you, and the orchestra will play for your entertainment.' He waved his hands and the orchestra began.

'We've got to start investigating, Squill,' said Tally. 'Let's go straight to B90.'

She moved towards the door but a waiter stopped her.

'You can't go inside yet, m'lady.'

Tally ground her teeth. She was desperate to search the corridor where she'd seen Allsop, maybe even check the cabin for clues. But the waiter would not budge.

'There are some advantages to being a servant and not a lady, Squill,' she said as the squirrel swung round and round on the railings. 'You can sneak anywhere you like and no one will bat an eyelid. Like Allsop does.' She ran her eyes over the decks below and caught a glimpse of another person, moving through the crowd freely. It was Charles. With his camera and tripod in hand, he looked very official. People were moving aside to allow him past, and he walked easily past a steward and through a door.

Tally looked out to sea. 'Three days till we get to New York,' she said. 'Three days till we can start hunting for Ma. But that means: only three days to catch this thief!'

CHAPTER SEVEN

'All clear!' came the call from the captain, several long hours later.

People slowly began to move away, heading towards the bar or the pool. But Tally was headed somewhere else.

'Finally!' she breathed, as she pushed through the throng of people and found her way to the corridor she had been in last night.

Tally walked past door after door until she came to cabin B90. The door to the cabin was open and Tally peeked in to see a maid kneeling down making the bed.

'Hello,' she said. The maid leapt up in fright. 'Sorry! I didn't mean to scare you.'

'That's all right, Miss,' said the maid. 'I'm just a bit jumpy.' She took a handkerchief from her pinafore and wiped away a tear. 'Everyone thinks I took the jewels. But I didn't, I swear it. They were just there on the table last night and ... then this morning they weren't. I don't know what happened.'

'When did you last see them exactly?' asked Tally.

'Let's see ... Miss Davenport decided not to wear her rubies to dinner because that set is too heavy. So the last time I saw them would have been around eight o'clock when my lady went to the dining room and I went to my own quarters. I stayed in my cabin all night then first thing this morning Miss Davenport called for me, accusing me of taking the jewels.'

'So they disappeared some time between eight o'clock last night and this morning?'

'That's right, Miss. But it weren't me!'

'I believe you,' said Tally. 'And what's more, I'm going to find the real thief!'

The maid smiled at Tally, though she didn't look convinced.

Tally left the cabin and walked back down the corridor, chatting it through with Squill as she went. 'Last night was when we saw Allsop outside that cabin!' she said. 'Oh, but I can't go making accusations until I'm sure. I might scare him away and never find the jewels or the Egyptian amulet. We have to *prove* it, Squill. Let's go and see what he is up to.'

Operation Hunt-the-Allsop began. Tally looked down every corridor, in every restaurant, on the decks, even in the swimming pool, but she couldn't find the steward anywhere.

As she popped her head in on the kitchens, she saw Mrs Sneed, sitting in an armchair. The chef was standing next to her, pouring her a cup of tea. *Well, that's nothing new,* thought Tally. But then she saw something she'd never seen before. Mrs Sneed smiled. Her face softened. Then the chef said something and she giggled – giggled like a little girl. Tally smothered her own smile and quickly walked on.

Down she went, lower and lower into the ship. It smelled smoky down here and her footsteps echoed on the wooden floors. About three flights down, she came across a sign on a door. It read:

CHIEF STEWARD'S OFFICE

Tally hesitated. Should she tell what she'd seen? She bit her lip then knocked on the door. There was no answer. She turned the handle – the cabin was empty. On the walls were charts and lists detailing the staffing plans, the ship's route, the meal times and cleaning rota.

One sheet held the holiday rota:

Special Leave Requests
Susan Pevensie – Thursday – to buy a wardrobe
~~Bert and~~ William – Friday – to go to Crompton
James Allsop – Saturday – to go to London
George, Julian, Dick, Anne and Timmy –
Sunday – to go camping

Tally's eyes widened. 'Allsop requested special leave to go to London on Saturday, Squill!' she said. 'That's the night the amulet was stolen!' Squill looked at her, his eyes wide too.

Tally scanned the cabin. Another piece of paper caught her eye. Pinned to the wall, it listed cabin numbers for staff. There, fourth entry down was:

Cabin D58 – Roger Taylor and James Allsop

'D58,' she whispered to Squill. She jumped back out into the corridor and shut the office door behind her. 'I think we should pay that cabin a little visit.'

'D45, D46, D47...' Tally counted the cabins as they went. Squill chattered on her shoulder, encouraging her on.

'D55 ... There – D58!'

Tally stopped at the door and looked left and right. There was nobody about. She couldn't go in. This was someone's cabin, not an office. But maybe it would be all right if ... if ... Before she could trouble herself about it, Tally put her eye to the keyhole.

There was Allsop! He was right by the open
porthole, standing in front of a wooden table with
his back to the door. He reached his hand into
his pocket and drew out something sparkly. Tally
breathed in sharply and momentarily lost sight
of the steward. She heard the sound of something
sliding on the table but by the time she put her
eye to the keyhole again, the sparkly something
had gone and Allsop was gazing out of the
porthole with his hands in his pockets, whistling
the same tune as before.

'Where did he put it, Squill?' asked Tally. 'It didn't go back into his pocket. It looked like he put it on the table, but there's nothing there.'

Allsop stepped towards the door and Tally dashed round the nearest corner. From her hiding place, she heard him come out of the cabin and lock the door behind him, whistling all the time.

'We need to get into that cabin, Squill.'

She walked up the flights of stairs to the grand staircase. There, she stood at the top.

'My corridor is off to the left from here,' she said to Squill. 'And Allsop's cabin is directly below this staircase, and off to the left too. I wonder. I wonder … Excuse me?' She accosted a passing waiter. 'Is there a plan of the ship anywhere?' she asked.

'Certainly, Miss.' He led her to the wall outside the Marconi room.

Tally ran her eyes over the diagram until she found cabin B58, her own cabin. She touched her finger to the map and ran it down two levels until …

'Oh!' She looked at Squill in triumph. 'My cabin is directly above cabin D58!'

She rushed to her cabin, fumbling with the key, then straight across the carpet and on to the balcony. A blast of cold wind hit her, fresh off the ocean. She leaned over the balcony.

'Allsop is two portholes down,' she said. She fingered the curtains, checking to see if they would make a good rope. They didn't feel very sturdy. Squill shook his head sharply, and Tally sighed. 'You're right, Squill. That really isn't safe. I don't want to fall in. I'd be lost at sea for ever.'

She sat down on her bed. 'There must be another way to get in.'

At dinner, Tally watched Allsop closely. He served everyone very politely, wearing smart white gloves. One of them was a little frayed at the wrist, the threads loose as if they had caught on something. Everything else about him looked normal. *But I saw him with something sparkly,* Tally kept reminding herself.

'How old is your daughter?' Mrs Montgomery asked Lord Mollett.

'Twelve,' he answered with pride.

'Goodness, I thought she was younger,' she said. 'She seems a little … wild …'

'We like her the way she is,' said Lord Mollett firmly.

'Oh, that's all very well,' said Mrs

Montgomery, 'but soon you'll have to find her a husband. You'll want the best, of course.' She stared at Tally, who was licking her knife to get the last bit of butter off. Hastily Tally put the knife down. 'I assume you've started Tallulah on the correct accomplishments?' Mrs Montgomery continued. 'Singing, painting, sewing? There's a wonderful book, you know, MRS PRIMM'S GUIDE TO BEING A LADY.'

Lady Beatrice gave a soft squeak. Her eyes opened wide.

'The best husbands demand such high standards,' continued Mrs Montgomery.

'The best will be someone whom she loves. And who loves her back,' Lord Mollett spoke up.

'But surely you'll be wanting at least an earl?' said Mrs Montgomery. 'Or a duke if you're very lucky.'

This was a touchy subject. Lady Beatrice had once been engaged to a duke. But he had called off the wedding when Lord Mollett was spotted walking out with a commoner, Tally's mother Martha. Lady Beatrice froze. Then she swallowed hard.

'There's more to life than decorum,' she said calmly.

Mrs Montgomery laughed and waved her hand airily. 'Oh, I know you Molletts don't stand on ceremony. You have conversations with *all kinds of people,*' she added pointedly. 'Now, Viola and I keep up with all the right sort. We go to London every weekend to see the museums and galleries. We even went to the British Museum last Saturday to see the Egyptian exhibition. There were so many wonderful pieces!'

'On Saturday?' Tally piped up. 'You were there on the same day as the burglary.' Tally looked at Mrs Montgomery closely. Surely she was far too silly to plan a burglary and smuggle an amulet out of the country?

'I know! I did the full quiz in yesterday's *Atlantic Bulletin* just to check I'm not the burglar,' Mrs Montgomery told the table. 'Turns out I'm definitely not. I don't own any clothes with stripes. I'm more of a floral person. Viola isn't the burglar either, are you, dear?'

'No, Mother.'

After dinner, as they all walked on the deck, Lord Mollett linked arms with his sister, and held Tally's hand.

'Ignore that horrid woman,' he said. 'Our little family is just right.'

Allsop walked by, whistling.

'What *is* that tune?' asked Tally. 'He's always whistling the same one.'

'Ah, that's an old folk song,' said Lord Mollett. 'It's called *My Bonnie Lies Over the Ocean*.' He began to sing it.

'My bonnie lies over the ocean
My bonnie lies over the sea
My bonnie lies over the ocean
Oh bring back my bonnie to me.'

He leant over the railing and looked out towards America.

Tally looked up at him. His forehead was

creased in a frown and his eyes looked sad. She squeezed his hand. 'We'll find her,' she said, and he turned to smile at her.

She held his arm as they walked back to their cabins.

Widdles was very excited when Lady Beatrice opened her cabin door. He'd forgotten that he'd only seen his mistress two hours ago and jumped out into the corridor and over her as if she was a long-lost love. Lady Beatrice laughed and cuddled him tight. Even Lord Mollett smiled when Widdles rolled on his back and barked.

'Very subtle,' he said, bending down to rub the dog's white fluffy tummy.

Tally sat down next to him and tickled Widdles's ears. 'Wait ... what's this?' She ran her fingers around his neck. 'He's lost his collar!'

A chill ran through Tally.

'Oh! Oh!' cried Lady Beatrice as she searched the floor of her cabin. 'It's not anywhere here.'

Tally looked at the cabin carpet. On the dark green wool there was a tiny thread of white. She bent down and picked it up.

Lady Beatrice was sniffing into her handkerchief. 'Tally, I loved that collar so much. He looked very smart in it. Where could it be? Could it have vanished?'

'I'll look for it, Aunt Beatrice,' said Tally.

She closed the door and headed back down the corridor. She knew where she'd seen loose white threads before!

CHAPTER EIGHT

'Mrs Sneed,' Tally whispered from the kitchen door. The housekeeper hadn't moved from her armchair.

'Come in, come in, dear,' she said. 'This is Chef Antoine.'

'A pleasure to meet you.' He bowed.

'This is Tally. I brought her up from a little girl,' said Mrs Sneed.

'How kind you are.' Chef Antoine stroked Mrs Sneed's hand.

'Well, you know what I always say …' She looked at Tally and waggled her eyebrows up and down.

'Um…' Tally floundered. "Make me a cup of tea'?'

'No!' Mrs Sneed gave a laugh. 'I always say, "kindness costs nothing".'

Tally nodded although she'd never actually heard Mrs Sneed say that. Ever.

'My Tally is very clever for ten,' continued Mrs Sneed.

'Twelve,' Tally corrected.

'Er ... twelve. I meant twelve.'

Tally looked around – there was Allsop, clearing plates. She moved a little closer, determined to get another look at his glove. Closer and closer she leaned.

He turned and caught her staring. Looking down at his glove, he quickly pulled his jacket sleeve over it. 'What are you doing here?' he said.

'I was just visiting my housekeeper,' answered Tally, 'and I noticed you'd caught your glove on something. It looks torn.'

'You need to leave,' he snapped. 'No passengers in the kitchens.' He frogmarched her out and slammed the door behind her.

Now what? thought Tally.

'Oh, I can't think without the Secret Library, Squill.' She sank into an armchair in the corridor. 'I need books!'

A passing steward heard her. 'If it's books you want, my lady, you could try the reading room.'

'Reading room?'

'Yes, it's just down past the post office.'

It wasn't the Secret Library but it *was* a library of sorts. Tally breathed in, smelling paper and wax and dust … and felt at home.

On the neat shelves were lots of books about ships and oceans. Tally thumbed past

The Arctic by Isa Berg

Ship Mysteries by Mary Celeste

The shelf below had books about sea creatures:

Seabirds by Alba Tross

Sharks by Meg A Bight

And below that was a more general shelf about animals.

Flying Animals by Flapp De Hoelway

Climbing Animals by Stig E Ness

Tally drew that one down. She sat on the floor with Squill next to her. For a second, as she opened the book, her heart hoped to see a hologram rise up. But this wasn't the Secret Library. The book stayed completely normal. Squill sighed in disappointment too, and snuggled on to her lap.

Still, the information inside was interesting. Tally learned that lots of animals are good at climbing. Bears and monkeys can climb trees, ants and spiders have tiny claws to climb rough walls and … Tally drew in a sharp breath…

Geckos!

She remembered the gecko in the Secret Library hanging upside down from a single toe.

'Squill!' she cried. 'If I had gecko feet, then I could climb down the side of the ship and get into cabin D58 … But how can I make gecko feet without the Secret Library?'

She slumped back down again.

It had always been the library that had taught her what to do: how to make a spider's web and a sniffing nose and even night-vision goggles.

'I can't make anything without the instructions. How will I ever be an inventor?'

At that moment the magic felt like a very, very long way away.

Tally closed her eyes for a moment, in despair. Then she sighed and pushed herself up wearily.

The daily bulletin was on the table.

ATLANTIC BULLETIN

from the Marconi Room

Third clue found in amulet case!

A shoe has been sniffed out by a police dog.

The item was discovered on the pavement
outside the museum.

'It's now clear how the thief got in,' said PC Bobby. 'He scaled
the wall and climbed in through the window. We think that's
when his shoe fell off.'

Police are now searching for an American in Southampton
wearing only one shoe.

p2 – Climbing gear: our fashion faves

Tally gasped. 'Allsop bought a pair of new shoes on Monday just before we sailed!' She pulled the receipt out of her pocket and showed it to Squill.

Then a thought hit her. *Charles. Charles had new shoes too.* She pictured him, swinging himself easily out of the sea with Widdles under one arm. In a trembling voice she added, 'And he'd be strong enough to climb up a wall.'

Tally stared at Squill. 'Surely it can't be him! It can't! Aunt Beatrice is so happy. And she's found someone who likes cameras just as much as she does.'

Charles's voice came back to her in that moment – '*One day, when I've saved up enough money, I'm going to open my own moving pictures company.*'

'Oh, Squill. I want it to be Allsop so much. I can't bear the thought of Charles being the thief. We have to get into Allsop's cabin and investigate. It's the only way to know.'

Tally sat on her bed watching the gecko climb up and down the walls. He made it look so easy. Squill patted her hand. He opened the cover of *Climbing Animals*. They'd borrowed it from the Reading Room to look at later.

'You're right, Squill. We should read a bit more about the gecko. See if that gives us ideas.'

Tally found the section on geckos.

'*A gecko has tiny scales on his foot,*' she read. '*The scales are covered in millions of tiny hairs, called setae. These are so tiny that they are invisible to the human eye.*'

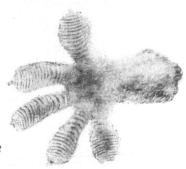

Tally's crested gecko darted onto the page, running across the book then jumping on to the bed post.

Tally turned the page

'*The setae are covered in pads and at the right angle, the molecules [8] in the pads attach to the molecules on the surface material.*'

'I see,' said Tally, thinking hard, 'so when a gecko is climbing a wall, a tiny, tiny thing in the gecko's pad called a molecule sticks to the molecules on the wall. So if our gecko has millions of hairs with millions of pads, he must stick very well. That's amazing!'

---

[8] Our bodies and everything around us are made up of teeny tiny things called molecules. In your body there are more molecules than you could count. Each molecule is made of atoms and has its own special shape. The molecules in your body cooperate to make your body work.

Squill lifted his own paw to look at it – just in case in the last few minutes he'd grown some of these incredible setae covered in pads.

'Oooh,' said Tally, 'it says here that the force that sticks the molecules together is called Van der Waals force.' Squill screwed up his face in concentration as he listened. 'When the gecko wants to move away, it changes the angle of its toe to break the attraction, and that allows it to unstick its foot.'

Squill jumped on to the side table, twisting his paws this way and that, trying to get them to stick on the wooden surface.

'If only we were in the Secret Library. Oh well, at least we've learned something from this book. Now we know about the force that makes the gecko's feet stick.'

But Tally's mind was still working.

'Squill …' she said slowly. 'I know we don't have the Secret Library's instructions, but do you think that I could *try* to make feet on my own?'

From the table, Squill's tufty red fur flopped up

and down as he nodded his head enthusiastically.

Tally drew and drew. She drew the gecko's foot and added tiny strokes for the setae. She drew a pair of hands, with tiny hairs on each finger. Then she traced around her feet and added more sketches of setae to the drawing.

'There,' she said. 'That's the design. But how do we actually make it?'

She had a pair of travelling gloves, in a soft leather.

'These would do ... and ... oh – these socks for my feet.'

But what about the hairs?

'Setae are super thin, Squill,' said Tally as she paced around the cabin. 'We know they are one tenth the size of human hair.'

She pulled at one of her curls. A loose hair came out.

'I need to make this thinner,' she said. She found the end and split it in half quite easily.

'That's split into two. But how do I divide it

even further?'

Tally fiddled with the hair between her thumb and her finger.

'Wuff!'

'Oh, Widdles! I told you not to play in the wardrobe. Now you've got your tail caught again.' Tally rescued him, pulling his furry tail free from a button. 'No wonder I'm having to brush you all the time. This is how you keep getting your fur tangled.'

She froze.

Widdles's brush! It had had lots of hair on it – a fine cloud of hair. Tally rummaged in the bin, full of paper from her discarded design drawings. Her hand found the hairy cloud and she pulled it out and spread it on the table.

'This might work!' said Tally in excitement. 'Your hairs are much thinner than mine, Widdles.[9]'

'Wuff,' he answered, looking proud.

Tally sewed all through the night, stitching

[9] A dog hair is about 25 micrometres (0.025 millimetres). Human hairs get thicker as you grow up. A child can have hairs of around 50 micrometres (.05 millimetres)

the cloud of fine hair on to the gloves and woollen socks. She didn't leave her cabin all the next morning. She missed breakfast, then she missed lunch. Lady Beatrice knocked on her door to check she was all right, and to bring her a sandwich, which Tally barely touched, and Widdles gulped down happily.

She kept going wrong: her first stitches were too big and clumsy and her hairs too wonky. But she kept trying and finally, by early afternoon, she had made hairy gloves for her hands and furry socks for her feet.

'I think that might be right,' said Tally. 'But we need one last thing to make them work.'

Tally closed her eyes for a moment. The Secret Library had taught her the magic she needed but would it work outside Mollett Manor?

She took a saucer from her tea set and placed it on the ground. Then she said the magic words:

'Gecko, gecko
My heart is true.

135

Help me learn
To do what you do.'

She sat back on her knees and waited.

There was a scamper from above, and the gecko darted down the wall and onto the saucer. When he jumped back away out of sight, he left a thin silver liquid shining on the little plate. Tally dipped her new gloves and socks into it. It was so thin and sparkly, like thousands of teeny-tiny diamonds.

'Let's test these gloves and socks, Squill.'

CHAPTER NINE

Tally took a deep breath. She pulled on the socks, put her fingers into the tight gloves, and stood there staring at the wall of her cabin.

How do I start?

She watched her friend the gecko. He just kind of jumped on to the wall, not worrying about not sticking, not thinking he would fall. The trouble was: Tally *did* think she might fall.

'It's my first proper invention, Squill,' she explained. 'The first one I've made on my own, with no instructions.'

She bit her lip.

'I guess I've just got to try, or I'll never find out. That's what inventors do.'

She took a step back and then, closing her eyes, she leapt straight at the wall.

Splat!

She opened her eyes again. To her amazement, she was held there, clinging on, two feet from the ground. The tiny hairs she'd sewn on to the gecko pads made a kind of electricity, fixing her fast to the vertical surface.

'It works!' she cried in excitement. 'My first invention works!'

Tally changed the angle of her fingers slightly and her hand lifted off the wall. She stretched it higher and higher and slowly she began to climb up. At first it felt really strange. Tally kept expecting to slide back down the wall, but she was firmly attached. She could go up or down, backwards or forwards and still she stayed on the wall. It felt amazing!

Now for the ceiling.

Tally gulped. She really didn't like the idea of hanging upside down, completely dependent on the force. But if she was going to risk climbing down the side of a ship, she had to be sure it worked.

Tentatively, she lifted a hand and put it on the ceiling. So far so good. She placed the other one next to it. Now she had two hands stuck to the ceiling, and two feet at the top of the wall. Her left foot shook as she lifted it and placed it next to her hand.

Squill looked anxiously from the ground. Not even he could scale flat walls and hang from ceilings.

'Here I go!' Tally yanked her other foot and put it quickly on to the plastered ceiling. Immediately it stuck.

'It works!' she said, hanging above the cabin.

She looked down at the room. She could see dust on the top of the four poster bed, and all the pictures hanging on the wall were distorted, their images upside down. The pretty patterned rug was clear from this angle. Before she'd just thought it was made of blue swirls but now …

'It's a peacock,' she realised.

She grew more and more confident and began to run about just like the gecko did, scampering on all fours from one end of the ceiling to the other, jumping on to the walls and back to the ceiling again.

'Whee! Look at me go!'

There was a knock at the door and, as quick as she could, Tally jumped down on to the floor and pulled off her gloves and socks.

It was Lady Beatrice.

'Are you all right?' Lady Beatrice wanted to know. 'I heard strange noises.'

'I'm fine,' said Tally, hiding her gloves behind her back.

'Thank goodness for that. You are very precious

to me, you know,' said Lady Beatrice.

Tally blushed.

'I'm just going to meet Charles. He's taking me for a stroll on the second-class deck. Oh, it's all so romantic!' she added dreamily.

'It is,' answered Tally with a smile, but inside she was thinking: *Please don't let Charles be the thief.*

Tally pulled back the curtains, and opened the balcony doors.

It was early evening and the sun was setting in the west, casting orange and gold on to the waves. She looked down. She could see the porthole below her, and the one below that, but the ship's hull curved so she couldn't see much beyond. Somewhere down there the ship met the water. A vision came into her mind of falling into the deep, deep, icy cold and she shivered.

Tally climbed on to the railings and stepped over the top rung. She was standing on the outside of the balcony now, the sea beneath her. She could hear the rush of the ocean, a hollow noise that pounded in her ears. Waves splashed against the hull of the ship as it moved through the water and a fine salty spray misted onto her face.

Squill jumped up and landed on her shoulder.

'Are you sure you want to come?' Tally asked. 'You don't have gecko feet.'

Squill wound one of her curls around his wrist, just in case.

'Hold on tight,' said Tally.

She placed a foot on to the wooden ship wall, then another, then her first hand, then her second.

She gulped hard. She was hanging on to the side of the enormous ship! She looked up to see another balcony above her. She could hear the orchestra playing and the distant clink of glasses as people had an evening drink.

She climbed down, past the first porthole.

The spray was stronger here, closer to the sea, and the wind pushed against her body as the ship cut through the water. Tally's arms began to quiver; climbing on all fours used a whole new set of muscles.

It was then that she had a terrible thought – she hadn't tested her gecko feet on a wet surface! She ground her teeth, cross with herself. *What if Van der Waals force doesn't work in strong spray?* Tally's heart beat faster. Her arms ached as the cold chill of adrenaline rushed through her body. It was only the thought of Squill clinging tightly to her hair that forced her on. She couldn't let her muscles fail! Squill wouldn't be able to grab on to anything to save himself.

Gritting her teeth, she carried on down, placing her feet and hands carefully. She counted down another level until she was hovering just above Allsop's open porthole.

Tally stopped to listen. The cabin was silent.

'I just want to look, Squill. I won't go into the cabin.'

She clambered down a bit more until she was perching on the rim of the open porthole. The table that Allsop had been standing in front of

when the sparkling suddenly stopped was right in front of her. She took off her gecko gloves and socks and, reaching in, she touched the wood of the table. The table top was divided into sixteen tiles of carved wood, set out in four rows of four to make a square. But one square on the third row was missing its tile.

Tally knocked on the table and listened.

'It's hollow, Squill. I bet there's a secret compartment in this table. That's where Allsop put that sparkly thing he was holding. I have a hunch Miss Davenport's rubies are in there. And Widdles's diamond collar. AND the amulet.'

She ran her fingers over the carved tiles – they shifted slightly in place. She touched the tile next to the missing square. To her surprise it moved easily to fill the empty gap.

'It's a sliding tile puzzle, Squill!' said Tally. 'The tiles can be moved into different arrangements.'

She began to slide the tiles, repositioning the empty square around the board.

'My guess is that when you have every piece in its correct place, the table will open. But how do we know where each piece goes? We'll never crack it! There must be millions of permutations.'

Sitting on the porthole, Tally leaned her head down to the table top, peering closely at the carvings.

'It's just squiggles, Squill.' She stared at the table top. 'It doesn't make sense at all.'

Tally was concentrating so hard on the puzzle that she forgot she was supposed to stay in the porthole window. She swung her legs down into the cabin and began to play with the tiles, slipping and sliding them about. The table top stayed fixed in place.

Tally cried out in frustration. This was impossible!

She leaned closer. The bottom left corner caught her eye.

'That looks like an "R",' she said. 'And that one could be a "T", and there's a "B"… it's letters, Squill!' Tally realised. 'Each tile has a letter, or parts of letters. When we arrange them right, the puzzle must make a word or a phrase. But what word?' She tilted her head to the side, scanning the cabin for inspiration.

Then she gasped. 'Look, Squill!' She pointed at a packet lying on one of the bunk beds.

It was a packet of chewing gum. Chewing gum labelled 'Juicy Fruit'.

'A sweet wrapper like that was found at the museum!' cried Tally. All of a sudden a harsh voice snapped:

'Who are you? And why are you in my cabin?'

CHAPTER TEN

For a moment Tally's heart stopped, thinking
Allsop had caught her.

But as she spun round she saw it was the other
steward, Taylor – Allsop's roommate.

'I'm sorry,' Tally stammered. She blushed
deep red. She hadn't meant to come fully into
the cabin, just to perch on the porthole. 'I ... I
shouldn't be here.'

'No, you shouldn't,' said Taylor. 'Thief!' he
shouted, and pulled an emergency alarm. Doors
opened and closed and there was the sound of
footsteps as people came running to help.

'No! No!' Tally cried. 'I'm not a thief.'

The alarm sounded. Tally covered Squill's ears

and put him into her cloth bag.

'What's all this?' Captain Roberts appeared in the doorway, looking very stern.

'I've caught the thief, Captain,' said Taylor. 'I found her in my cabin. I have no idea how she got in but there's no doubt she was planning to steal something.'

'No, please, listen!' Tears filled Tally's eyes.

'Take her down to the brig,' said the captain sternly. A moment later, Allsop came rushing through the door too, and put his hand on Tally's arm.

A crowd had gathered, coming out of their cabins and down from the floors above when they heard the ship-wide alarm. A man pushed his way through.

'Wait! Wait!' It was Lord Mollett.

'Pa!' cried Tally in relief. 'Help!'

'Unhand my daughter,' Lord Mollett ordered Allsop. 'She's not a thief ... Let her explain.'

Allsop reluctantly removed his hand.

'Thank you,' said Tally, rubbing her arm. She

stepped back until she had a bit more space. 'I promise I'm not the thief. But I think I know who is.'

There was a gasp from the crowd. Everyone made themselves comfortable to listen to her – some passengers sat on the floor, some leaned against the wall.

Tally coughed to clear her throat. 'On Monday night, I saw Allsop going into cabin B90. What were you doing there?' she asked him.

He shrugged. 'I was just checking everything was all right,' he said.

'But that's *my* corridor,' said Taylor in surprise. 'Miss Davenport is my guest.'

'I … I heard a strange noise,' said Allsop defensively.

'The very next day, Miss Davenport noticed her rubies had disappeared. She thought it was her maid.' Tally glanced at the crowd. Everyone was staring at her, entranced by the tale.

'Then I saw Allsop admiring our dog's diamond collar.'

'So?' said Allsop. 'It's a pretty collar. And the diamonds are two carats each.'

'You seem to know a lot about it,' said the captain, narrowing his eyes slightly.

'Our dog is very excitable,' Tally went on. 'He likes his collar. I expect he wasn't too happy about you taking it off him. Indeed, I found white threads on our carpet.' She drew them from her bag. 'White threads that are missing from ...' – she pulled back Allsop's jacket sleeve – '... here!' Everyone stared at Allsop's torn glove.

A lady fainted in shock in the corner of the cabin.

'That little dog...' grumbled Allsop.

'But,' Tally continued, 'it's not only Miss Davenport's rubies and Widdles's collar that have been stolen.'

Everyone looked at one another, puzzled.

'Tell the little girl to speak up,' came a voice from the crowd outside the door. 'We can't hear her at the back.'

'I think our thief here is the same person who stole the Egyptian amulet that went missing from the British Museum on Saturday night.' She stared at Allsop.

'But that's impossible,' said the captain. 'The thief is in Southampton. He's American. And he's only wearing one shoe.'

'Allsop, you went to London on Saturday,' said Tally, ignoring the captain's points.

Allsop shrugged.

'You did,' said the captain. 'It's on the rota.'

'And you have Juicy Fruit chewing gum.' Tally held up the packet. 'Gum that someone travelling back and forth to America could easily buy. Gum left at the scene of the crime.'

The captain drew in a sharp breath.

'And what's more ...' said Tally, '... you are wearing brand-new shoes!'

Tally pointed to the tag on the bottom of Allsop's shiny black brogues.

The captain stepped closer to Allsop and placed his hand on the steward's shoulder. 'Now listen, Allsop, what's going on? Explain yourself, man.'

'This doesn't prove anything!' Allsop responded. 'Lots of people like Amercian sweets. Lots of people buy new shoes before a sea crossing. And it was this girl who was in *my* cabin.'

The captain turned to Tally. 'Well?'

Tally swallowed hard. Allsop was right. She had no proof. Hadn't the knitting lady had American sweets? And Charles was wearing new shoes too. She was ready to give up – except …

'There's something else,' she said to the captain. 'Something I saw through the keyhole yesterday,' she confessed, blushing. 'I saw Allsop holding something sparkly. Then the next second it had disappeared. I think he put it inside that table,' said Tally, pointing to it.

'Nonsense!' said Allsop confidently. 'That's just an ordinary table.'

'It's hollow,' said Tally. 'And if you lift it … Pa,

can you help me?' Together the Molletts jiggled the table and it rattled.

'You see!' said Tally. 'There's something in there.'

'Open this table!' the captain ordered Allsop.

'I don't know how,' lied Allsop. 'It's not my table. I've never seen it before. Gosh, who put that table there?'

'It IS your table,' said Taylor slowly. 'I remember, three years ago, on our first voyage, you brought that table with you and set it up there.'

'If you can't open it, there's no proof,' said Allsop smugly.

'He's right, m'lady,' said the captain. 'You need to open this table now.'

Tally bit her lip. She had to work out the code. The solution couldn't be random. It couldn't. It had to mean something to Allsop.

The steward grinned smugly. He crossed his arms, a satisfied look on his face. He was so pleased with himself that he began to whistle.

'There's that song again,' said Tally. 'You're always whistling the same tune.'

Allsop turned pale. 'No, I'm not.'

'Yes, you are. Pa – how does it go?'

'My bonnie lies over the ocean,' sang Lord Mollett.

The other passengers joined in –

'My bonnie lies over the sea,' they bellowed. They put their arms round one another and sang out loud and strong –

'My bonnie lies over the ocean … Oh bring back my bonnie to me.'

Allsop started to shake.

'It's the key!' Tally cried. 'That song is the key!'

'How does it work?' asked Lord Mollett.

Tally looked at the table top again.

She saw three 'B's, a 'G', a 'T' with half an 'O', a bit of a 'K' and a bit of a 'C' and 'M'.

'The words of the chorus!' she cried. 'The letters make the chorus – "Bring back my bonnie to me".'

'Oh, well done!' cried Lord Mollett.

Allsop gave a little sob.

'But the song is split across the four lines,' Tally said. 'It's very clever!'

She began to slide the tiles into place.

'The "B", "R", "I", "N" and "G" make "bring" for the first line,' she said, fitting them together. 'Then the next line is "back my". Then "bonnie". Nearly there now.'

'But where does the empty tile end up?' asked Lord Mollett.

'Haha!' said Allsop. "You'll never work it out.'

'I'm not certain,' said Tally. 'But my guess is that it goes last. It would be too hard to remember if it went in the middle.'

'Oh,' said Allsop in disappointment.

'So the last line is "To me" and then a blank space, which gives us… 'Tally stood back.

There was a loud click.

Lord Mollett pulled apart the two leaves of the table and there, shining for all to see, were:

Miss Davenport's rubies

Widdles's collar

And a necklace with a round gold pendant.

Tally looked at the necklace closely. *Could this be the missing amulet?* she wondered. Either way, it certainly didn't belong to Allsop.

He was the thief all along! And Charles was innocent! Tally beamed in relief.

'Take Allsop to the brig,' ordered the captain. 'The police will deal with him when we arrive in New York.' Taylor took Allsop out of the cabin and then the captain turned to Tally. 'Thank you,' he said. 'I'm sorry I didn't believe you at first. Allsop has been on my crew for three years. All that time, little items of jewellery have gone missing. We always thought the pieces had just been lost by careless passengers. But now, thanks to you, I know the truth.'

By the next morning every passenger on board knew that Tally had solved the fiendishly difficult puzzle of Miss Davenport's missing rubies. People came up to her all day to congratulate her.

Most astonishing of all, Viola found Tally by the railings. 'That was wizard!' she whispered in admiration. Then she shut her mouth quickly and walked away before her mother saw.

Tally felt a warm glow inside her. She had invented something useful and she had solved a puzzle.

'And I did it without the Secret Library,' she whispered to Squill. Suddenly the world seemed full of possibilities. Even when she finished being a Secret Keeper she could carry on learning and inventing for the rest of her life!

Miss Davenport kissed Tally on both cheeks. Lady Beatrice clipped Widdles's collar back on and he ran about happily in it until he fell over his ears. Twice.

The captain called Tally and Lord Mollett to the bridge to look at the pendant once more. The bridge was right at the front of the deck, and it looked forward over the sea. In the centre was a large wooden wheel for steering the ship. Captain Roberts let Tally have a quick go at holding it and it hummed in her hands. She grinned up at him.

Then he laid the round pendant on the table. It

was old: a ring of gold holding a dark yellow jewel. Tally peered closer – it wasn't exactly a jewel, she realised. It was some kind of amber and inside was a small beetle. She tilted her head. She recognised the beetle from somewhere. She'd seen drawings of it once in the Secret Library when she'd looked up the pyramids.

'Is that a scarab beetle?' Tally leaned in. 'Scarab beetles were worshipped by the Egyptians.'

'If it is, then this pendant really could be the missing amulet!' cried Lord Mollett.

'I don't know anything about beetles,' said the captain. 'But I know who does. Take it to the American Museum of Natural History in New York. They can check it for you and if it is indeed the missing amulet, they can contact the British Museum from there.'

'Good idea,' said Lord Mollett. He took the pendant and wrapped it in his handkerchief, then smiled down at his daughter. 'Well, Tally, looks like we've got our first stop in New York sorted at least.'

CHAPTER ELEVEN

It was their very last morning on ship.

Excitement was in the air as everyone packed their bags ready to go. Tally and Lord Mollett were helping Lady Beatrice cram her three remaining hats into her bag when there was a knock at the door. It was Mrs Sneed.

'Begging your pardon, my lord, my ladies ...' She was twisting the fabric of her pinafore anxiously.

'What's the matter, Mrs Sneed?' asked Lord Mollett.

'It's just that Chef Antoine has asked ... he has asked me to stay with him here on the ship. For ever.'

'Goodness!' said Lady Beatrice.

'Yes. I've been on my own since my Arthur died all those years ago and so – I said yes. I'm going to be a ship's cook. Well, actually, I'm going to sit in the armchair while Antoine cooks, but still ...'

'That's wonderful news!' said Lord Mollett. "We'll have to replace you, I suppose. What exactly did you do at the manor house, again?'

'Not that much,' Mrs Sneed finally admitted. 'It was all done by Tally here.'

She reached down and gave Tally a hug. For once Tally didn't know what to say.

'Thank you, Tally,' said Mrs Sneed. She stood up, cracked her neck ...

Creeaaak craaack

... and was gone.

'Well,' said Lady Beatrice. She sat down hard on the bed next to Widdles (who had pulled a hat out of the bag and was chewing its feathers). 'Mrs Sneed has gone and made a new life for herself. A whole new life with someone she loves.' She looked into the distance, lost in thought. 'Just like that.'

'Ready to go?' said Lord Mollett. He fished the hat out of Widdles's mouth and pushed it into the bag.

'I suppose so,' said Lady Beatrice with a sigh.

'Of course!' Tally was so ready she could barely keep still. Somewhere out there was Ma. They were closer to her than ever.

'We'll go straight to the museum,' said her father, 'drop off this piece and then go to every hospital, every record office, every register system. We won't stop till we find her.'

'Wait … wait just a moment,' said Lady Beatrice. 'Actually, I'm not ready. There's something I have to do … Someone …' and she picked up Widdles and dashed out of the cabin in a cloud of feathers.

'We'll meet you by the gangplank!' called Lord Mollett after her.

Tally and her father leaned over the ship's railings, desperate for their first glimpse of New York. Squill did three somersaults round the top rail but he still couldn't get their attention. They were too busy staring as the ship slowly sailed up the Hudson River.

'That's the Singer Tower.' Lord Mollett pointed to a building with a rounded top leading to a point. 'I think it's the tallest building in the world.'

'Everything's so big!' Tally had never seen so many tall buildings. 'Skyscrapers' they were called, her father told her.

The SS *Voyager* pulled alongside the pier. It was packed with horse-drawn cabs waiting to collect people, and friends and family waving to greet their loved ones. Noises filled the air – people shouting, horses neighing and stomping, the sound of horns honking. Tally shivered in excitement. She couldn't wait to get out there and find Ma.

One by one the passengers walked onto the gangplank and down off the ship.

'There you are!' The knitting lady came rushing up. Squill dived into Tally's cloth bag as fast as he could. 'I've finished these for your kitten.' She handed Tally four frilly purple booties.

'Thank you,' said Tally politely. 'He'll … love them.'

'Kitten?' asked Lord Mollett when she had gone.

'Don't ask,' said Tally.

Tally, Lord Mollett and Mr Bood waited for Lady Beatrice.

Soon there was hardly anyone left on board.

'Where is she?' said Lord Mollett, looking from side to side.

There was the patter of heels and Lady Beatrice came running, hand in hand with Charles. Widdles scampered along next to them, nearly tripping them up.

'We're getting married!' Lady Beatrice cried all in a rush. 'Charles and I are getting married!'

'Oh, Beatrice, that's fantastic!' Lord Mollett picked his sister up and swung her round. 'Congratulations, Charles,' he said, shaking the man's hand.

'Thank you,' he said. 'We're going to be very happy.'

'Wuff!' said Widdles, hoping for a bit of attention too. Lady Beatrice scooped him up.

'We're going to Los Angeles!' cried Lady Beatrice. 'To a place called Hollywood. It's only small but lots of filmmakers are gathering there to experiment with cameras and moving pictures.'

'That sounds very exciting,' said Tally.

'Moving images?' said Mr Bood in glee. 'I fancy I might be of some use.' He puffed out his chest and turned from left to right, waggling his face so Charles could see what a wonderful actor he could be.

'Oh yes, you must come too, Mr Bood,' said Lady Beatrice. 'I can't possibly cope without you.' She waved him towards her luggage.

Lady Beatrice bent down and hugged Tally close. 'I'll come home for the wedding,' she said. 'I need your help choosing the right dress.'

'Maybe there'll be something in MRS PRIMM'S GUIDE TO BEING A LADY,' Tally suggested.

'Oh, that silly book,' cried Lady Beatrice.

'I don't need it any more. I've got much more important things to think about now. Charles and I are going to put Hollywood on the map!'

Tally hugged Widdles. 'I'm going to miss you,' she said, as the puppy chewed one of her curls. Squill solemnly put a paw on the dog's head as if to say 'farewell'.

'See you soon!' called Lady Beatrice as she walked down the gangplank with Charles, Widdles in her arms. Mr Bood waddled after them carrying the luggage.

Then it was just Lord Mollett and Tally left.

'Shall we?' he said, holding out his arm.

'Goodbye,' Tally whispered to the ship as they set off into New York.

Squill held tight to Tally's little finger as the hansom cab jiggled and joggled along the street, bouncing up and down with the rhythm of the horse. Brie and the gecko snuggled down further into Tally's cloth bag.

Their driver was Irish. He had sailed over from

Cork many years ago.

'This is a city of dreamers,' he told them over the rattle of wheels as the horse turned along the west side of Central Park. 'Everyone comes here to make their fortune.'

It was quieter here, away from the bustling main streets full of restaurants and people and trams and horses. Tally could still hear the rumble of the elevated train that ran high above the shops and streets, but now there were fewer carriages and motorcars trundling by.

On her right, Tally could see couples walking arm in arm in the park and children running in the grass.

On 77th Street, the cab pulled up outside the American Museum of Natural History. The building was a soft red, with two large turrets at either end. Tally and her father climbed the steps up to the entrance.

'We'll be as quick as we can, Tally. Let's just drop off this pendant and go. If it is the amulet, they can send it back to London.'

Tally nodded. Normally she would be over
the moon to be inside a real museum – but at the
moment, all she could think of was Ma. She was all
twitchy and jumpy, desperate to start their search.

Tally's shoes click-clacked on the museum
floor. The hall before them was filled with large
glass boxes, holding dioramas of stuffed animals
and birds. She paused by a display while Lord
Mollett spoke to an attendant.

'*The Andean Condor is the largest bird of prey,*'
Tally read from the sign. Squill gave a squeak
as he stared at the enormous bird. Its wingspan
was over three metres. 'That's double my height,
Squill!'

The next glass box held butterflies and
caterpillars. Tally had made a chrysalis before,
using instructions in the Secret Library. She'd
seen holograms of all the different tropical
butterflies, but here were their bodies and wings
right in front of her. She pressed her nose to the
glass, smiling at the yellow Peacock Pansy, a
specimen from South Asia.

'Doctor Silva curated that exhibition,' said
an attendant beside her. 'It's one of our most
popular dioramas.'

'It's fascinating,' said Tally.

Lord Mollett joined her. 'Well, Tally – it seems
you really did save the day! They think this *is* the
missing amulet from the British Museum. We
just need to pop up to the library to see someone
called Doctor Silva, who can identify the scarab
beetle and confirm it for sure. Apparently he
knows all about insects,' said Lord Mollett as he

and Tally headed off towards the stairs.

'She,' the attendant called after them.

'Excuse me?' said Lord Mollett, turning back.

'She – Doctor Silva is a woman. Doctor Martha Silva. She's one of our top curators. She's from England actually, like yourselves!' added the attendant, with a big smile.

Tally stopped dead in her tracks, then turned slowly on her heel.

Martha … From England … In the library …

It couldn't be. Could it? She looked up at her father.

Lord Mollett turned to face her, his shocked expression mirroring her own. She felt for his hand and held it tight.

CHAPTER TWELVE

Tally's heart was beating so fast it was making her dizzy.

She followed Lord Mollett up the stairs to the museum library, Squill perched behind her ponytail.

'Don't get your hopes up,' said Lord Mollett as they turned a corner. Tally didn't know if he was talking to her, or only to himself.

Click-clack, click-clack went Tally's shoes on the floor.

There was a door at the end of the corridor. Lord Mollett went first, pushing it open.

The library was bright and airy, with large windows and a skylight overhead. At one of the desks was a woman with dark curls. She was surrounded by leather-bound books, absorbed in reading. Even though the lady's face was hidden, Tally knew. She knew.

This was the moment Tally had been waiting for her whole life. But all at once, with her goal so near, she felt utterly overwhelmed. Her courage deserted her, and her knees went weak. She slipped behind her father, hiding from view.

Lord Mollett's head was fixed straight ahead. His voice shook as he spoke her name –

'Martha.'

The woman looked up. Her face turned white. She looked frozen in place

'Bear?' she said slowly. She shook her head as if she couldn't believe it. 'Wh … what on earth are you doing here?' She stood up abruptly.

Tally was still trembling. What if Ma didn't recognise her? What if she didn't want her? Squill touched her neck with his paw; a tiny soft stroke for luck, and for strength. Tally took a deep breath. She stepped out from behind Lord Mollett and watched Ma's head turn.

Ma's eyes widened and she dropped her pen. Her knuckles were white as she held tightly on to the desk. Ma took a shaky step in her direction, and another.

'T … Tally…?' she said hesitantly. 'My Tally … ?'

She held her hand to her mouth and gave a little cry. She stumbled forward and in an instant she crossed the floor of the library. She swooped Tally up in her arms. She smelled musky and warm. She smelled like … like bedtime stories and birthdays and walks in the forest. She smelled like: Ma. A thousand memories flooded Tally's mind.

'Mummy,' she whispered.

'I thought I'd lost you,' Ma cried, her voice muffled in Tally's hair.

'No, *I* lost *you*,' Tally corrected. 'But we found you again.' She reached for her father and drew him into the hug. Squill settled on Ma's shoulder.

There they stayed, the four of them, for a very long time, until finally, with a sigh, they drew apart and smiled shyly at one another.

Then they held hands and paw, and together they stepped into their future.

Acknowledgements

My thanks go: to Lena McCauley and the team; to James Brown for his fantastic illustrations; and, as always, to my wonderful agent Eve White.

I am also in debt to the American Museum of Natural History, for kindly answering all my questions and sending me old photos and layouts.
— Abie Longstaff

ABOUT THE AUTHOR

ABIE LONGSTAFF is the eldest of six children and grew up in Australia, Hong Kong and France. She knows all about squabbling and bossing younger sisters around so she began her career as a barrister. She started writing when her children were born. Her books include *The Fairytale Hairdresser* series and *The Magic Potions Shop* books. She has a life-long love of fairy tales and mythology and her work is greatly influenced by these themes.

Abie got the idea for *The Trapdoor Mysteries* from her parents' house in France. The house is big and old, with lots of rooms and outbuildings. In one of the bedrooms, there is a secret entrance hidden in a fireplace. It leads to a room that was used by the French Resistance during the war. It was the perfect idea for a book!

Abie lives with her family by the seaside in Hove.

ABOUT THE ILLUSTRATOR

Inspired by a school visit from Anthony Browne at the age of eight, JAMES BROWN has wanted to illustrate ever since. Having won the SCBWI's Undiscovered Voices 2014 competition, he had illustrated the *Elspeth Hart* series and two of his own *Archie and George* books. Two picture books he has written, *With My Mummy* and *With My Daddy*, are recently published and his first author-illustrator picture book, *Jingle Spells*, is out as well. He is the illustrator for *Al's Awesome Science* series. James comes from Nottingham and has two cheeky daughters who usually take off with his favourite crayons.

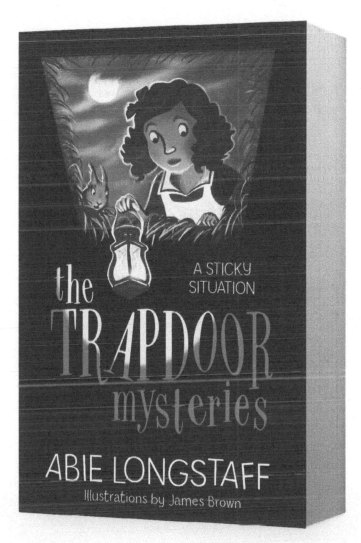

THE SCENT
OF DANGER

the
TRAP
DOOR
mysteries

ABIE LONGSTAFF
Illustrations by James Brown

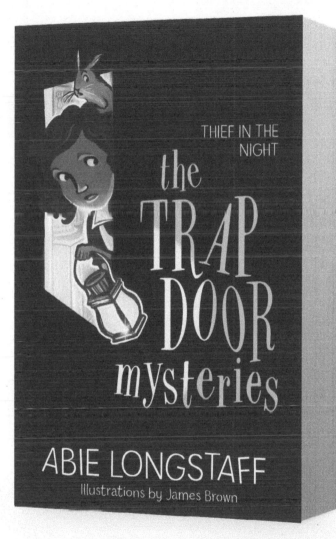

THIEF IN THE
NIGHT

the

TRAP
DOOR

mysteries

ABIE LONGSTAFF

Illustrations by James Brown